put it on me

A BBW EROTICA

PENNY BLACWRITE

contents

penny blacwrite's catalog

Joyride: When Loyalty Kills
When a Wife's Fed Up
When a Wife's Fed Up 2: Kalena's Revenge
When a Wife's Fed Up 3: Kalena's Redemption
Christmas in Vegas: On Cloud 9
Toxic: A Forbidden Romance
For Every Black Woman's Soul: A Poetry Medley
For Every Black Woman's Soul II: A Poetry Medley
Loving All of Me: A BBW Love Story
Charlie's Angels: A Polyamorous Affair
Charlie's Angels II: A Polyamorous Affair
Toxic II: Generational Curses

*Click on the links and it will take you directly to the Amazon
page to download *

note to reader

Thank you so much for supporting my very first independent novella. An autographed copy of this book can be purchased on my website at www.pennyblacwrite.com, which also comes with a custom bookmark. The genres are Romance, Erotica, and Women's Fiction. It's a great balance between Romance and Erotica. A true courtship romance, not instant love. Also, keep in mind that erotica is not just a book full of sex. Erotica consists of three major tenets; anticipation, arousal, and action (sex). I did my best to explore all three tenets while telling a great story of budding romance, providing a satisfying and explosive ending with the reveal of some mind-blowing secrets, the Penny Blacwrite way. Enjoy!

connect with penny b

Stay connected with me on all platforms.

acknowledgments

Editor: C Wilson https://www.authorcwilson.com/

Cover Design: P. Wise Productions https://www.prettiwise.com/

Model: Jelissa Turner https://www.instagram.com/lisssaturner_/

synopsis

Eva Castler has been abstaining from sex for a little over a year after falling out badly with her ex, Jared. As a BBW sexy fitness influencer, she's used to men lusting over her and just wanting her for her body. She's not only celibate to avoid creating soul ties with meaningless people, she's harboring deep rooted trauma from her past relationship. The last thing she wants is to give herself to another ruthless man who refuses to truly commit.

That is until she meets GQ in the most abrupt way. Instantly sexual chemistry dances between them both, causing Eva to question her abstinence. GQ is fine, established, and a loving single father to a fifteen year old girl named Gianna. Masculine and a true alpha, GQ seems like the perfect man on paper, but he too is dealing with deep rooted trauma from his past relationship.

Will these two allow their undeniable chemistry and intense romance to bring them closer, or will the secrets from their pasts cause them to drift away from each other?

LOCKED OUT

EVA CASTLER

"You got that big ass mansion over there and ain't nobody blowing your back out in one of those many bedrooms? It's been three months since you moved into your dream house, girl. Drop that celibacy shit and get you some dick!" My best friend Nika buzzed in my ear, bugging me on the other end of the phone.

It hurt to admit that she was right. I had been practicing celibacy for a little over a year. More like sixteen months and seventeen days to be exact. Celibate by choice of course. I mean, it's me; Eva, The BBW Diva. I have ten million followers on Instagram and twenty-eight million on TikTok. I'm also a top 1% OnlyFans creator and plus-size influencer. I could easily have any man at my beck and call, throwing me against the wall and sliding inside my wet juicy plum, but the truth was I was still on a hiatus from men after I fell out badly with my ex over a year ago.

The last thing I needed was a headache dealing with one of these broke-ass, inadequate niggas. With that said, I was determined that until the right man came along, basking in singlehood and self-love was my remedy. Nika knew that. She was just being her pestering self, probing and pricking me because she truly believed if I didn't get some dick sooner or later, I'd dry up like a prune. I could understand her logic if we were pushing forty but we were thirty-two and wasn't shit old and dried up about me just because I wasn't having sex.

"You know a regular sex life is good for your health, Evena." Nika chided, her sarcastic banter playful in spirit and intent.

With the phone pressed between my ear and neck, I giggled along with her before taking a deep breath and exhaling.

"Yes, I know. But I'm just not ready." I pouted, before stepping out of my plush King size bed and fixing the G-string that was snagged deeply up my ass. "And besides I like my peace. Not only do I not need the drama but I also don't even need a man in my life right now!"

Nika sighed dramatically, her huff totally exaggerated. "Yeah, yeah, yeah. That's what all of you independent modern women say."

I took a look around my room, which was where I slept and created content. With four ring lights scattered on each corner of the room, and two tripods centered in front to capture every angle I swayed on my platinum chrome baby, it sure looked like a studio. Sexy, durable, and newly installed, my pole was what set me apart from the other plus-size content creators.

"But seriously, though. I want for nothing. Anything extra

around the house that I need, I hire help. Trust me, when I say I'm good. I'M GOOD!"

Nika snickered loudly. "Oh please. So, who do you hire to come and wax that ass? Because it doesn't matter how many vibrators you use for that clit, Ms. Rose can't make your body do the things that a tall, chocolate dog with a horse for a leg can."

Strutting past my stripper pole, I laughed hysterically as I stepped into my closet, looking for the perfect outfit for tonight's pole dancing class. When I first started doing them, they were live, but now that I've hired a fancy videographer, I can pre-record my routines and send them to him to make a variety of visual content for me. From Instagram, Facebook & TikTok reels, clips for OnlyFans, and full-length videos for my website, he did it all. I especially loved it, because I didn't have to interact with crazy fans who didn't appreciate my artistry as fitness and were adamant on sexualizing it.

"Nika, you're hell. But I'll have you know that my rose does just fine. See unlike you, who can't keep her kitty to herself, I refuse to just choose any ole man to lay down with just to say I'm getting some. Shame on you hoes!" I chided.

Nika sucked her teeth so loud, I could hear her tongue pop. "Says the bitch who sells videos of herself half naked twirling on a stripper pole looking like a rotisserie chicken."

"A juicy, plump, well-seasoned rotisserie chicken, might I add." I joined in on Nika's laugh, my cackle a tad bit lower than hers.

Almost instantaneously, my room turned pitch black. The lights from my ceiling and my ring lights blew out. Quickly, I looked outside my window and noticed that even the driveway light was off.

"Siri, take me to the Ring App," I yelled aloud, now pacing in circles around the perimeter of my bed rug.

"Everything alright over there girl?" Nika inquired.

My body was jittering and my hands were shaking, as I tried to calm myself down from panicking.

"Yeah, everything's okay. I think."

"What you mean you think?"

"My electricity went out," I said, suddenly shaken.

"Where? In your room?"

I scratched my head. My anxiety was building faster and faster. "Yeah, but it also looks like it might be dark in the whole house. The lights for the driveway are out also."

"Well, put on the flashlight from your phone, make your way to the control panel, and play with the breakers."

My brows crunched inward as I squinted my eyes, trying to comprehend all that Nika was saying.

"You don't know where the control panel is do you?" Nika mocked.

I cracked an embarrassed smile. "No, I don't Shanika. And what are breakers?"

"Shaking my head Evena! This is exactly why your ass needs a man! Like I said, you got that big ass house over there and don't know what to do. Fuck, it's almost midnight, I can't call Troy over there to help you. Remind me again, who the fuck told your ass to move all the way out to Marietta!" Troy is Nika's brother. I've known him as long as I've known her; nine years. They were the first people I met when I first moved to Atlanta.

As I fumbled with my phone returning my attention back to the Ring app, I was brought to an error message that said the cameras were disabled.

"FUCK!" I yelled.

4

"What now?"

"My ring cameras are disabled," I told Nika as I wobbled towards the bed in the pitch dark, in search of my lace robe.

Thump!

"Ooohhh, shit, fuck!" I hollered out in agony, as I hopped on one foot while leaning forward with the bruised foot in my hand. Stroking it continuously, I inhaled and exhaled several times.

"Girl, are you alright?" Nika buzzed in my ear. I was so frustrated, that I wanted to rip the Airpods out my ears and throw them across the room.

"No bitch. I'm not alright. I can't fucking see." Georgia was notorious for not having any lick of light outside. Even high beams couldn't fight this damning darkness.

Irritated, I cut my phone flashlight on, stormed towards my bed, and picked up my lace robe. I tied it on, found my slippers, and made my way out of the room, following behind every flashlight beam.

It was interesting that as soon as the lights went out, a spooky type of silence came over the entire house. I headed towards the garage, looking for my larger flashlight, when I heard a loud hiss that caused me to jump immediately.

"E, you good?"

"I think so."

"You think so? That doesn't sound too promising. You want me to call the police?" Nika shuddered and I heard the panting rise in her inflection, which caused me to panic.

I hadn't been in this house for a full one hundred days and the thought of calling the police didn't sit well with me. As I neared the entrance of the garage from my living room, the hissing noise progressed along with a scatting sound.

Thump.

A vibration bounced off the wall from inside the garage. My throat clogged up as I gripped my phone tighter. My heart was beating so hard that I could hear its rhythm clearly inside my head. Hesitantly, I inched closer and closer towards the garage, illuminating the darkness with my phone's flashlight. As soon as I got to the entrance of the empty garage I didn't even house my car in, the hissing sound returned and a small round figure jetted across the room.

"Ahh, ahh, what the fuck!" I yelled.

"That's it girl I'm calling the police!"

Darting the flashlight all over the room to find my enemy, I finally came across him, a furry creepy crawler with teeth as large and haggard as long ice sickles. I hopped back quickly and ran in the opposite direction, dropping my phone and falling out of one of my slippers.

"Eva. Are you okay? I'm calling 911."

I sprinted through the house towards the front door, directly out to the curb. The door slammed behind me, and it wasn't until the cold January air hit me that I realized I was officially locked out of my house with no phone and one shoe.

"No. No, don't call the police. It was just a rat. One of the biggest rats I've ever seen.

Laughter erupted on the other end of the call. "Girl, you're from New York. Rats run your city. I know you ain't let no rat run you out your house."

"How'd you know?"

"Cus I can hear your fat ass out of breath."

"Stop laughing Nika! I'm telling you that was the biggest rat I've ever seen. He had long, big teeth and was hissing."

Nika sucked her teeth and chuckled. "Girl that wasn't a rat.

That was a possum. And yeah I'd run away from one of their asses too."

Catching my breath and tightening my lace robe, trying to restore some warmth, I exhaled, and a large pool of carbon dioxide belted out of my mouth.

"Shit, it's cold," I complained as I walked back towards my front door. "Nika, can you find me a 24-hour exterminator? I know they have them out here with all these insects and bugs."

"Exterminator? Bitch are you crazy? That can wait. I'm finding you a 24-hour electrician to come and put your lights back on."

"Ok, hurry up." I urged her as I fumbled with the door knob. "Girl I'm locked out of the house with no phone and one shoe." I sighed as I continued shaking the door knob. "Thank God for AirPods unless I wouldn't still be on the phone with you. I dropped my phone in the house."

"Damn girl."

Sucking my teeth and scratching the side of my head, I turned around, eyeing my BMW. "Luckily, I don't lock my car door. I'm gon' go sit in there."

"Good. It shouldn't be long. Duke Electrical Services. He already responded to my message in the 24-hour emergency chat on his website. What's your address?"

"2405 Doraville Lane. Marietta, GA 30063"

Shivering from the beating cold, I settled into my car seat.

"Booked. He'll be there in an hour and a half."

I held my head up with my mouth wide open and groaned. "Fuck. The last thing I remembered was my phone being on twelve percent. My phone's gon die" I scoffed.

"Well, ya ass won't be able to use it anyway but to talk to me since your phone is locked in the house, and you're using your

Air Pods. So sit tight and wait for your knight and shining armor, Mr. Gideon Duke."

"You done background checked the nigga already, Nika?" I gasped.

"Nah. His name and picture are on his website. Gideon Duke. Born and raised in Guyana, West Indies. 34-year-old master electrician with sixteen years' experience in the industry, having worked for the federal government half of his career and the other half running his own business." Nika recited mechanically as if she was the host of a popular dating show.

I sighed, irritated as fuck that I was outside half naked with a G-string on and a lace robe and one fucking slipper.

"I'm freezing my ass off, and you out here trying to play matchmaker."

"Ahh shut up. Nobody told you to run out of the fucking house with no clothes on. Now put yourself together for that fine-ass man on his way to you. He's tall and handsome, but he has dreadlocks and I know that you're not really into that but give him a chance."

"Goodbye Nika. I'll call you when I get back in the house."

"Goodnight chica. Stay warm and toasty for your Adonis."

"Whatever, bitch," I sassed, before taping the side of my Air Pods and ending the call. With no phone, no keys, no shoes, and no clothes, I wrapped my arms around myself clinging to the ounce of body heat I had left. An hour and a half couldn't come any faster.

two

BREAKING & ENTERING

EVA

L oud, insistent taps startled me from my sleep. In a frenzy, I hopped up and there he was, tapping on the window. He stepped back, allowing me to get a better view of him. Even from outside of the car, and in the dark of the night, it was clear to see that he was one tall, fine, handsome motherfucker. He was so fine that I didn't mind the dreadlocks. They actually fit his style.

Locking eyes with him felt magnetic, to the point, that I instantly became self-conscious. Remembering that I was half dressed, my hair a mess, and I probably had drool down the side of my cheek from how hard I was sleeping, I lowered my head in shame as I gathered myself to get out of the car.

He backed up slowly as I pushed the car door open. Stepping out onto my bare foot, his eyes went straight to the ground.

"You good?" He asked as he stepped forward, extending his hand for me to grab onto.

Latching onto his arm, I felt his strength immediately. The weight of his arms felt like boulders. It was obvious he worked out faithfully. He pulled me up in one quick motion and there I was, exposed. No bra on, a G- string, with a thin white lace robe draped around my double fupa, with most of my ass out. The cold air caused my nipples to harden and his eyes went straight to my cleavage. A gleam of sparkle flashed in his eyes before he caught himself and motioned his gaze back to my face.

"No, I'm not good. Forgive me, but I've been having a terrible night. My electricity went out and I went to my garage looking for a flashlight when a possum chased me out of the house. I was so scared that I forgot that I had a slam lock on the door. I had my friend call you and I've been sleeping in the car since."

Closing the car door behind me, never letting go of my hand, he motioned me towards the sidewalk.

"Sounds like you've been through it."

"I have."

"Also sounds like you're gonna need a locksmith since you're locked out of the house."

I sucked my teeth so hard, as frustration built inside of me. "FUCK! I totally forgot about that." I yelled, jerking away from him.

He grabbed me back quickly, not allowing me to break from his grasp. As I turned to face him, a sly smirk rode up his mouth. "Chill out ma. I got you." He said, his baritone cool, smooth, and gentle.

He guided me towards the front door and pulled out his phone. He pulled up an app and began typing ferociously. A minute later, he scanned his screen along the Ring camera attached to the wall near the entrance and my door unlocked.

I stood there stunned, with my mouth ajar as I watched him walk past me. "How did you do that?"

"Don't worry about it. Just get your ass in the house and show me to your control panel." He demanded. This time he wasn't smiling. His angular face was as stony as a statue while his eyes pierced through my robe.

I walked inside, following his flashlight until the door slammed behind me. I took a few steps forward, embarrassed to admit that I didn't know what the fuck a control panel was. I turned around to face him and caught him licking his lips. His phone's flashlight scanned me up and down, bringing attention to all of my goodies. He had me under a microscope. I felt so naked in front of him.

"Can I change first?"

"No, you can't." His words were sharp and curt. He meant business.

Nervously, I snickered. "What? Mr. I need to change first. Then I can show you to the control panel." I insisted. Now I was getting a bit annoyed.

"Nah. I prefer the view in front of me. Go on. Show me to the control panel."

His gentle, yet firm request turned me on. Talking to me like that, he could get anything from me. Refusing to argue with him, I turned back around and walked forward until I neared the back wall.

"You don't know where the control panel is at."

I chuckled softly. "Nah, I don't."

"Take me to the garage."

Facing him again, I shook my head nervously. I pointed

towards the living room." I'm not going over there, but you can. That's where the possum was at."

"You gon' go wherever I tell you to go." His aggression was sexy but becoming alarming. Images of the many episodes of *Law & Order* and *Criminal Minds* flashed through my head. Was he even an electrician? He didn't have any tools on him and although there was a work van wrapped with his logo sitting outside, didn't mean he was all the way legit.

"Are you this aggressive with all of your customers?" I inquired.

"No, just you."

I blushed, and I was happy it was dark and that he couldn't see it. That was until he flashed the light in my face.

"Go on. Show me to the garage so I can watch your sexy ass walk away."

Was I dreaming? This man wasn't shy at all and he didn't take no for an answer.

Doing what he said, I walked through the living room, making my way toward the garage. Once there, he moved me aside and rushed to the left wall. Watching him strut confidently in the garage without fear, settled my anxiety a bit until the hissing sound I heard nearly two hours ago returned. I became jittery but it was obvious that he was unbothered. Within two minutes all of the lights in the house came on and that's when I saw them.

There were now three huge possums surrounding him. As much as I wanted to run, I couldn't stand to leave him all alone to get eaten alive by these deadly creatures. In a flash, he turned around and without warning, he pulled out a small compact gun and fired three clean shots knocking the heads off each possum. Three faint swishes replaced what I knew as a gunshot. He must have had his silencer on. Blood and guts splattered across the room as he stormed in my direction.

"I'm heading to my truck to get my tools. By the time I'm back, there should be three trash bags on the couch." I was starting to notice that he was very forceful. He didn't ask me anything, yet he told me everything.

"And don't even think about changing those fucking clothes. I'll be right back!"

INTRUDER

GIDEON "GQ" DUKE

Tonight had to be one of the luckiest nights I've had in a long time. It wasn't just because pussy was sitting on a platter waiting for me. It wasn't because I was about to get paid nearly twelve hundred dollars for less than an hour's worth of work. To be in the presence of Eva was something I had never seen coming in a million years. From following her on Instagram & subscribing to her OnlyFans, I knew she lived in Georgia, but I never thought that I'd run into her, especially not like this.

The fact that she was more beautiful in person without a face full of makeup turned me on. Not to mention, she was so fluffy and dainty. Her mannerisms, her coy smile, and the fact that she didn't resist me, despite how feisty I got with her intrigued me more. So although her Pandora's Box was wide open, I still wanted to dance around it before devouring her.

As I threw a bunch of tools in my box just to pass the time, I tried to calm my nerves. Not many women made me nervous, but Eva was different. From the first time I saw her on Instagram, she captivated me, to the point that I had to subscribe to her OnlyFans. I felt so embarrassed because my boys Ice and Twan clowned the fuck out of me when they found out I was a faithful, and loyal subscriber. I can't lie, doing so made me feel like a simp. My boys and I vowed that we would never be one of them suckers making these hoes rich, but even from the phone screen, there was something so alluring about her.

As a Caribbean man, I've always had a thing for a fine BBW, and not one of these BBL action figure-built BBWs. I'm talking about the real BBWs who are proud of their fupas, who have soft skin, nice feet, and edges. BBWs who are fit and healthy but not overly obsessed about losing weight because they rather maintain it. And that was Eva. I knew it from watching her twirl on the pole and dedicate herself to working out for the last two years I've been subscribed to her.

Just the thought of her chocolate skin melting into the pole as she swirled, twirled, and gyrated up and down and all around the pole, had me stuck. I couldn't get the image of her round shapely body as she took control of my entire phone screen, bringing me into that alternate reality of hers. Whenever I watched Eva, it felt like only we two were in the room. Through whatever digital device I had at my disposal, whether a phone, tablet, or computer, I could feel Eva in my presence. Meanwhile, she was less than thirty feet away from me, and somehow I was scared of what I'd do next. This was a moment a nigga like me dreamed of and yet, I was stalling in my truck, waiting for the right moment to return back to her home to clean up that damn mess.

Palms sweating and my heart beating, I grabbed my extra

toolbox and jumped out of the van. The sun had risen and a bitter chill permeated the air, reminding us that Atlanta's two months of winter were in full effect. Considering that it was January, we'd have a few more weeks of choppy cold and brutal winds before the weather fully bloomed into spring. As I approached her door, I took a deep breath and exhaled. Although a woman as sexy as Eva intimidated the fuck out of me, I couldn't let her see me sweat.

Upon entering the house, I found Eva sitting on her white leather couch. Her knees were plastered together as she bounced her feet up and down. Anxiety was written all over her face but she was still wearing the white skimpy negligee that I demanded she remain in. A satisfied smirk rode up my lip as I charged toward her and picked up the black garbage bag seated on the side of her. My eyes never jolted. I continued watching her, admiring her chocolate essence.

"She follows instructions. I like that," I teased, finally breaking the silence, as I shook the plastic trash bag open.

She sucked her teeth and brushed her toes together. I smiled at her nervousness and peered down at her toes which were painted a soft pink, complimenting her skin tone. Even her ankles were sexy.

"He's quite demanding. I don't really like that," she responded sarcastically. She was witty. I liked that.

I chuckled, as I slid past her glass end table towards the door leading to her garage. The black of her pupils followed my every move. "Yes, you do," I said.

Just as I left it, the brains and guts from the two possums were still splattered on the floor of the garage. I knelt down, pulled my heavy-duty gloves out of my back pocket, and shoved my fingers inside. The sound of footsteps and the smacking of lips approached from the side, and there she was; heavenly looking with big pouty lips and breasts large and bountiful, I just wanted to drink from her fountain until I completely depleted her.

"In fact sir… Mr. Gideon, I don't. I don't appreciate how aggressive you've been. Do you usually conduct business like this with your clients?" Duck lips took the place of her sexy pout as she folded her arms.

I wanted to chuckle again, but I didn't want to further upset her. I just found it entirely funny that she would even think I'd behave like this with other clients. If I did, I'd certainly be out of business. That's how I knew that even though Eva sold the illusion of sex for a living, there was still a warm ditzy innocence about her. She didn't truly understand the power of her sexuality and just how much it turned me on if she really thought my expressed interest in her wasn't totally exclusive.

"Of course not," I answered meekly as I picked up the head of the possum and tossed it in the garbage bag.

I stepped away from the bag grabbed the broom and dustpan burrowed in the right corner and started to sweep up the rest of the bloody guts.

"Arrgh," Eva roared. "Blood is all over my floors."

A low whistle rattled from my throat as I shook my head. "Relax baby girl. I got it. I'll clean all of this up for you."

She exhaled, unfolded her arms, and placed them on her hips, which brought more attention to how fat her pussy was, and no it wasn't her fupa. I knew the difference. From the outline of the negligee that cut into her crotch, it was obvious that her pussy was plump, fat, and tender.

"Oh thank God. Don't worry, I'll pay the extra clean-up fee just for your help." Eva lowered her gaze from the wall that she used to avoid looking directly at me. I could feel the nerves travel from her collarbone to the tip of her fingers.

"Don't worry about an extra fee. Consider it on the house, a solid."

"Thank you. I appreciate that." Scratching her chin, she tilted her head to the side, her mouth slightly open allowing me to fully assess her soft kissable lips. "How much do I owe you in total? And do you take Zelle because I don't have any cash?"

After I dumped the dustpan into the garbage bag, I dusted my hands on my dark denim jeans. Prying the gloves off my hands, I faced her completely, slanting my gaze.

"I just told you, it's on the house."

Eva stumbled backward, nervousness etched all over her body and shook her head back and forth. "Not charging me to clean up is one thing, but I can't let you do this entire job for free," she protested, a twisted pout on her mouth and accompanied by an exaggerated pose and her hands on her wide hips, again.

"Who said anything about free?"

As I tied the garbage bag together and tossed it to the side, I noticed how tense Eva's soft face had gotten. Panic flowed through every crevice of her pretty profile, from the corners of her eyes to her nose and her lips.

"Uh, I don't know what kind of woman you take me for, but I make too much money to fuck for a service that I can pay for," she sassed as she rolled her eyes and sucked her teeth.

Attitude.

It turned me on even more to know that she wasn't a pushover or the type to just go for anything.

I chuckled, revealing all of my teeth and I instantly noticed her face soften. "I take you for the kind of woman that knows her way around the kitchen."

She sucked her teeth even louder. "Why because I'm fat?"

I reached forward and grabbed her wrist. "No. Because your kitchen is decked out with all the latest appliances and you have a double oven."

Instantly, she smiled.

"And besides the only word I'd describe you as is sexy."

Silence but the heaving from Eva's chest rang through the room as our exchange intensified with our stare. Tired of waiting for her to respond, I stepped closer, admiring all of her body.

"You've been in this all night. Go change into something even sexier and come and make me some breakfast. That's how I'd like you to pay me for my services. Oh, and don't forget to throw on some heels to match."

four

STRANGER IN MY HOUSE

EVA

As much as I wanted to resist, argue, and fight him on his request- I mean demand, I couldn't. While it seemed and sounded crazy that this man, a complete stranger would ask me to cook breakfast for him in lingerie, it didn't feel too crazy. The truth was, I loved to cook, especially for my man. My ex, Jared, loved my food and bulked up in all the right places- his arms and back from my cooking. The only problem was that Mr. Electrician wasn't my man. I didn't even know his ass.

So why did I feel comfortable with his request? So much that instead of combating him, I bit my bottom lip and turned on my heels. I could feel him watching my every move, as I made my way to the open staircase. Taking a deep breath as I ascended each step, my nerves were getting the best of me. The closer and closer I got to my bedroom, the more I started to feel like I was making a big mistake.

What message was I sending if I cooked for him in lingerie rather than just paying him for his service? Thoughts of my mother reminding me to be on the lookout for predators raced through my head. The vow I made to myself to dodge all fuckboys who just wanted sex or categorized me as easy because of my profession raced through my mind simultaneously. I swore to myself that after Jah and I broke up, I wouldn't give my body to another man who hadn't proved to me that he was worthy of my time and most importantly that he saw me outside of my profession. Which explains why I haven't had sex in over a year.

It didn't matter how much money they made, it seemed like every man I had run into either had baby mama drama, was a womanizer, or worst; conniving, sneaky, and downright trifling. Dating in Atlanta wasn't for the weak and before I convinced myself to sell my beautiful mansion, pack up to move back to overcrowded and just as saturated New York, abstinence, celibacy, or whatever you want to call it was my remedy.

Inside my walk-in closet, which was illuminated with LED drop lights that could be manipulated to the brightest and the darkest shades, I rushed to the innermost corner where all of my frisky outfits and props were organized into bins. My body was shaking as I fidgeted through the drawers. Breathing in and out, I couldn't believe that I was ready to succumb to the demands of this stranger.

What the hell was I thinking? Was it because he was one of the most attractive men I've laid eyes on in Atlanta? Despite having dreadlocks, which I despised, everything about him exuded masculinity. He was tall, and dark, with big hands. He knew how to carry a gun, and it was safe to say he had the ability to protect me. Was that the reason I was ready to risk it all and tempt my celibacy? Because he saved me from two possums?

Come on Eva. Your standards have to be higher than that!

Unable to stop my rambling thoughts from consuming my mind, I pulled out my phone. It was on seven percent after I spent most of my battery using my AirPods talking to Nika last night since my phone was stuck in the house while I was locked out. I dialed Nika's number quickly, as I knew she'd give me her honest opinion, and that was what I needed more than anything.

Within three rings, Nika answered.

"Everything all good girl? Did he do a good job?" She asked immediately.

I don't know why but I lowered my voice to above a muster. "Girl. This man is crazy. He's insisting that instead of paying him for his service, I cook him breakfast in lingerie and heels!"

Nika sucked her teeth so loudly, the sound almost resembled a screeching tire. "Shhhhhh, girl what!"

Gripping the phone so close to my ear, I sighed. "Yes. Girl, this man is crazy. Talking about I look like I know my way around the kitchen."

"Well, you do. I must admit, even though you're from up north, yo ass can throw down. You better gon' head and feed that man."

Twisting up my mouth and scrolling my eyeballs to the top of my orbs, I kissed my teeth.

"I can't believe you're encouraging this shit. I don't know this man. And the fact that he's so damn aggressive makes me think that he's some kind of sex addict or that he does this with all of his clients. I'm about to just pay him two grand and send him home. I don't have time for this bullshit."

I could hear Nika rolling her eyes and sucking her teeth

through the phone. "Girl, you don't have time for shit but making content and complaining about not having a man then acting like you don't want or need one when it's obvious you do. And here this fine ass man comes into your life and you're pushing him away."

As I ruffled through my wall bins pulling out a few different negligees, I fumed and cleared my throat. Nika was so thirsty for any bit of male attention, that she couldn't see a red flag if it were in her face. Her color-blind ass would mistake it for orange.

"He came into my life to do a job, Nika!" Scrunching my nose, I continued, "He's not some fucking Prince Charming. He wasn't sent from God. He's just a horny fuckboy like the rest of these niggas tryna slither his way into some good good." I ranted. I was becoming frustrated that Nika couldn't see what was clear as day; he was trying to take advantage of me.

"OK, and? So what if he's tryna get some pussy? He's a man. You're a woman. That's just the nature of this shit, girl. And the truth is you need some dick. Loosen the fuck up!" Nika advised.

I fumed so loud, that a grunt rumbled from my throat. I was so tired of hearing Nika tell me that I needed dick like that was the antidote to all of my fucking problems. I needed more than dick.

"You better stop growling and go jump on that man. Channel all that aggression over there guh. Let him knock the stiffness out yo ass."

"Shanika, at this point in my life, dick just ain't enough. I need more."

Just as I made up my mind that I wasn't adhering to his sexist charade, I found the nude negligee with the diamond-crusted G-string that I'd been looking for this whole time.

"Well if you don't give him a chance, you'll never know if it could ever be more," Nika suggested.

"Right," I replied sarcastically, letting the final syllable linger on.

Nika huffed and puffed, fuming through her nose, I heard the attitude all in her tone. "Listen, bitch! I don't know what the fuck your problem is, but wake up and smell the fucking coffee. You're a sexy BBW that does Only Fans for a living, and you're acting all prude on some celibate shit after that bullshit with Jah. Girl it's been two years, you've got to move on."

"Whatever," I pouted.

Nika sucked her teeth loudly, the hiss was crisp like a rattlesnake's.

"Get off my phone Evena, and go put it on that fine ass man. You've had his ass waiting long enough. Got this man coming over your house and you half-naked already, girl you better act like you know what's up."

"But—"

"But nothing. Bye, girl!"

Click.

That was the end of the discussion. I threw my phone down raised the negligee to my chest and sighed. Biting on my bottom lip, I was so conflicted. On one hand, I knew what Nika said had some truth to it, but I also knew how I felt in my heart about the kind of man that I wanted this time around held more weight for me. Although I did Only Fans, my content was strictly fitness-based. The fact that I was using the pole made it sexual and it didn't matter how I explained it, people always looked at me as just a stripper, IG, Only Fans hoe. Despite that daunting reality, I still had an inkling of hope that the man made for me would accept and respect my profession as a content creator and model, and see that I deserved real love. I didn't care what Nika thought.

Yet, I couldn't get him out of my mind. The audacity of him to protect me, and want to screw me, make love to me, and do whatever else he saw fit. The nerve of him to swoop in and force me to notice him, and even demand that I cater to him. As I closed my eyes, and allowed my mind to wander to parts of my imagination I hadn't explored in a long time, I smiled. It was obvious that what he wanted most was intimacy. To request that I make him breakfast in lingerie rather than overpay him for thirty minutes of work, told me all I needed to know, giving me the extra pep in my step and sway in my hips to slide into my negligee, spray some perfume and slap my glossiest lip gloss on and do exactly what Nika instructed; go and put it on that man!

five

FALL FOR YOUR TYPE

GQ

Twenty minutes later, Eva's strappy-heeled sandals ascended down the open-view stairs, one after the other. Her skin was glistening and her calves were sculpted and firm. From the soles of her feet, my eyes scanned up her body slowly, taking every curve of her in. The nude ensemble she wore fit her body so tight, that it looked like it was painted on and melting into her skin. Consequently, the contrast between her chocolate hue and the nude lingerie made my dick hard.

As she came down the stairs, her body's solidness was inevitable. She carried her weight well and she knew how to walk in them high-ass heels. Strutting forward with confidence and boldness that turned me on, I licked my lips and bit them slowly.

"Damn!" I had to stop myself from squealing like a fan, but

truthfully, I was a fan. An OG fan, dating back to her secret webcam days, that no one really knew about.

"You look every bit of edible, gorgeous." I couldn't help myself from showering her with compliments. She looked refreshed and relaxed. There was just a different type of glow to her than earlier and I was happy to bear witness to her illumination.

She bit down on her bottom lip and side-eyed me. "Thank you."

I held out my hand, ready to grab her by the wrist and waltz her toward the kitchen. She had other plans. Completely ignoring my hand, she stepped in front of me and kept walking. Her strut, which was really a graceful glide had me in awe. The motion from her hips produced the gyration that bubbled down her ass, all the way to her thighs. Eva was a brick house. She was plump and solid, just how I preferred my women, and most importantly, her confidence bloomed through the room.

I pressed the crotch part of my jeans down, determined to conceal my budding erection. She noticed immediately and darted an irritated sneer my way. I chuckled because it was obvious that although she decided against her gut to cook for me, anything more wouldn't come easy.

"What you about to feed me, woman? "I inquired as we entered the large open-layout kitchen with three separate marble islands, all of the latest stainless steel appliances, and a fancy Samsung fridge off in the corner.

As she looped around the large rectangular island, running her index finger along the edged marble stone, she clicked the tongue and titled her head, "What do you want?"

"Hmm, it depends. Are we talking about American

breakfast? Wait, aren't you from New York originally? You don't have any West Indian in you?"

Eva scrunched up her face and raised her brow. "How'd you know I was from New York?" she questioned suspiciously.

I bit down hard on my lip, completely forgetting that she had no idea that I had been watching her on Instagram for years and knew all the basics about her. I knew that she was from Brooklyn originally and stayed out in Atlanta once she graduated from Clark Atlanta University. Her food recipe reels on TikTok revealed that she loved Caribbean music and loved to cook all different kinds of cuisines. I always wondered if she was West Indian, although she never said so.

"Everybody from New York dun forward dung hea, suh." I clarified quickly, to hide the fact that I was indeed an obsessed creepy fan.

She cracked a fake smile yet never softened her eyes. I wasn't sure if she believed me or not, but there was no way I was about to spill the beans that I was a secret admirer.

"You're right about that and you're right about me being from New York. Born in Brooklyn, and raised in Queens but no I'm not West Indian. I'm a real Yankee," she explained, exaggerating her New York accent, which always turned me on.

I appreciated the diction in their voice rather than the country drawl and southern twang most Atlanta women had. In my years of dealing with women from Atlanta and women from New York, I found that New Yorkers usually had stronger vocabulary. Talking to a New York chick, always felt like I was getting hip to some game or some new shit.

"I like that. Well, as for me, I was born and raised in Guyana, West Indies. I moved here when I was eighteen."

"I know!" she asserted as she pulled a few things out of the fridge. Balancing a tube of I Can't Believe It's Not Butter, eggs, spinach, and oat milk in her hands, she motioned toward the island and placed the items down. Licking her lips, she circled me with her eyes.

"And how did you know that?" I asked.

Eva's body jerked forward, her nipples pressed against her negligee as she fought to keep her nerves under wraps. "I actually read your bio on your website," she mustered before rubbing her hands together. Batting her lashes, she looked at me softly allowing me to admire her hooded-shaped almond eyes. "Gideon Duke. Born and raised in Guyana, West Indies. 34-year-old master electrician with sixteen years' experience in the industry, having worked for the federal government half of his career and the other half running his own business," she spit off almost mechanically, but in a sexy whisper.

I couldn't help but chuckle. Here I was embarrassed about knowing who she was, when her ass had probably Googled me, been on my social media and all. The fact that she read my seven-paragraph bio and could rattle off a portion that crisp and clean was refreshing.

"Impressive," I praised. I was so used to pretty bimbos who weren't very articulate. Eva was different. Yeah, she was a sexy piece of eye candy, but she was smart and sharp, which I already knew from Instagram, but experiencing it in person just reaffirmed it, making me want her more and more. I wouldn't let up on the pressure at all. My eyes danced around her succulent melon breasts to the nape of her neck and down the curve of her spine. I stepped closer to her, invading her personal space, and took a deep breath. I needed to smell her. Her scent was light and airy.

"So tell me something, baby gal. Where your mon at?"

While I may have known more about her than she even knew, I always wondered how in the hell her fine ass was single. She looked good, had her own, had no kids, and was college-educated. The fact that no man had swooped her up yet was unbelievable.

"The fact that you've somehow convinced me to cook for you in lingerie, should tell you that I'm single." Her sassiness was sexy, just like the curvature of her back and how her double-caked ass sat high and heavy.

"I'm sure that's by choice. I can only imagine your roster."

She cracked two eggs on the edge of the island, dropped them into a bowl, and whisked them together before dashing a sprinkle of salt and pepper in the mixture. Raising her brow and side-eying me, she pursed her lips together.

"Could you imagine me being celibate, because my roster is non-existent?"

I narrowed my brows and licked my lips. "No, I can't imagine you being celibate."

"And why's that?"

I stepped closer and closer until I was submerged in her burnt coconut scent. She was so damn edible looking and I was hungry as fuck, ready to feast on her all night. "Come on. Do you see yourself gal?"

Her body language had relaxed and her shoulders dropped. Bating her eyelashes, she smiled. The softness in her eyes gave me the permission I needed. I placed my right hand on her left ass cheek and stretched my fingers, clenching and caressing her tender, smooth bubble ass.

"Woyy gal, look bamzy." I snickered, laying my GT accent on thick as I smacked her ass hard enough it stung my hand.

She jumped, and bit her bottom lip, holding back a smile.

"The real question is where's your girl at, and how would she feel about you trying to seduce me?"

I searched her eyes. I needed her to feel me as much as I had felt her.

"I'm not trying to seduce you."

"Of course you are!"

Stepping forward, I wrapped my arms around her waist, nuzzling the tip of my nose into her neck. She smelled so good and her skin was so smooth.

"Is it working?" I asked.

She started to squirm in my arms, as she rubbed her hands against my wrist. Her touch was magnetic and I couldn't resist, so I went in for the kill and bit softly on her neck. I couldn't help myself. I had to taste her. Swirling my tongue around her neck, I trailed up to her earlobe and sucked on it and the magical word *yes* escaped her mouth.

I gripped her tighter by the belly, holding on to the firmness of her body, as I continued sucking on her earlobe. She allowed my tongue to explore all of her upper body from the neck, her ears, and collarbone until she struggled to break away from my embrace. I refused to let her go and held onto her tightly.

We were now playfully fighting for control, but I let her win, as I could feel the goosebumps arise on her skin. She broke away from me and the intensity in her eyes grew, sinking its claws into my pupils.

"It's a little hot in here," Eva said, as she picked up her phone from the other edge of the island. Seconds later, air from the high ceiling vents came blasting out with low music accompanying it.

I watched Eva go into panic mode, opening and closing the fridge and filling up her arms with several ingredients before placing them back on the island. I studied her every move, from how she diced bell peppers into perfectly sized bites, to how she ripped open the pack of turkey bacon so carefully.

"While I'm not too big on swine, I'll have you know that if I eat bacon, it has to be pork bacon."

Without responding, Eva twirled backward into the refrigerator, opened it, and pulled out a pack of Oscar Meyer Applewood bacon. Soft melodic tunes of Tony, Toni, and Tone danced through the house, setting the perfect mood for lovemaking. I bobbed my head steadily. It was a nice revelation to learn that she enjoyed R&B music as much as me.

"So, Mr. Gideon."

"Call me GQ," I said.

She blinked three times then tugged on her bottom lip. "Okay then, GQ. How come you're single?" she asked, her whisper barely above the music.

"Give me your phone!" I ordered.

Raising her brows and shifting her tongue to the corner of her mouth, it was obvious that she was confused.

"Why?"

"Just give it to me."

Without any more backtalk, she passed me her phone and I pulled up YouTube and punched in the letters for the song that would show her better than any word I could say.

Jamie Foxx's voice crooned through the speakers, as he sang the lyrics to a song I resonated with so much.

"Tell me why I always fall for your type," I sang along to the classic song, as I stepped even closer to her and circled my index finger on the top of her right breast. She sucked in her bottom lip and twirled her tongue around her sexy mouth.

"And what type is that?" she asked.

I lowered my eyes, glancing over her body, and rubbed my

hands together. "Sexy, and alluring with a complex past and history."

"Hmm, what makes you think I have a complex past?" The veins around her temple popped out. I could tell she was on edge.

"We all have a complex past," I said as I motioned my hand from the top of her breast to her areola. Pulling on her thick budding chocolate kisses of a nipple, I felt my wood stiffen. "I believe in people like youuuuuuuu," I sang the words of Jamie Foxx's song "Fall For Your Type" that played in the background, as I absorbed her coconut scent and swirled my tongue around the ridges of her areola.

Here we go again.

She jittered, bouncing her shoulders up and down, squirming in my embrace, as she pushed me away. As she struggled to break free, I whispered in her ear, "Relax."

At the sound of my voice, she instantly complied, and my hands began to wander down to her soft tummy, lower to the peaks of her fupa until they landed right on her fat pillow-like pussy. She squeezed her thighs together in a timid motion. My instant reaction was to palm her pussy tighter. A moan escaped her mouth as my lips descended her neck, leaving a smooch on each speck of skin until I reached her collarbone.

Eva was gyrating and whining her hips as I made my way to the inside of her plum.

Niagara Falls.

I looked up and we exchanged glances for a brief moment until I kissed her. So damn full of heat, I could barely control myself. As our kiss deepened, and my fingers became drenchingly damp and pruney from the wet secretion of her treasure, her squirming became more pronounced. I could taste her moans in my mouth as she blew out hot and bothered breaths.

The more she pulled away, the more I fought for her until I felt a forceful push.

Now, with our hot and heavy embrace broken, we stared at each other with heavy, confused eyes, not saying a word, until she finally broke the silence.

"I think you should leave. This has gotten way too out of hand."

Pursing my lips, I nodded my head. I refused to fight her on it because she was right. If she hadn't stopped me, I would have gone full beast mode, fucking her tender ass all night. But the truth was although I never penetrated Eva, I felt like I already explored her sexually. I wanted to know her beyond the sex appeal, beyond the OnlyFans, and her newfound fortune. So I did what was best, which was to turn on my heels and leave quietly. But by no means, did I surrender. Things weren't over between Eva and I.

FANTASY

EVA

As much as I wanted him, as much as I wanted to give in, I just couldn't. It didn't matter how good it felt, I had to remind myself that he was a stranger. The nerve of him to just waltz into my house, and try to seduce me. It was the most uncomfortable yet satisfying encounter I've had in at least two years. But I couldn't just give in that easily.

I spent the last year abstaining from all kinds of sex, including masturbation. There was a time when I thought I could masturbate and still be celibate, but I realized I was cheating myself and lying to myself. I knew that for me to be successful on my celibacy journey I had to starve myself of all sexual gratification. So three months in, I ditched the porn, stopped masturbating, and even unfollowed so many of the overly sexual OnlyFans girls on Instagram. Many of them I worked with in the past on collaboration promo videos but the more my content became fitness and lifestyle-oriented, and less sex, me and four of my best IG baddie friends grew apart.

And although I missed them, I had to admit that the lack of their influence in my life made it a whole lot easier to be celibate. With that said, I couldn't just abandon my celibacy because a handyman came to do his job. Besides the fact that he was sexy, alluring, and literally saved my life from a gang of possums, he didn't do shit to deserve a piece of this kitty kat.

Content with the decision I made, I smiled to myself, as I prepared a very much-needed bath. Tossing Epsom salt and three small bath bombs into my Jacuzzi whirlpool tub, I watched the water turn into a concoction of lavender, powder pink, and baby blue. The aroma of relaxation hit my nostrils, as I stepped out of my silk robe. After the crazy night I had, I just needed some self-care and me time.

I settled into the tub, the warm water submerging me under the bubbles. Leaning forward, I grabbed the bottle of Moscato from the charcuterie board that was upholstered on the tub topper and poured myself a glass. In a matter of seconds, I sucked down the entire drink and it was everything I needed to wind down from the roller coaster of a night I had. Luckily, today was an off day for me. I didn't have to shoot any content. I didn't have any meetings with my team or any other big companies that wanted to bring me on board as a brand ambassador until next week. Ashley Stewart recently pitched the idea of me hosting their annual pageant and Essence wanted me to run a workshop for plus-size fitness content creators, amongst a heap of other things.

As I poured myself another glass, a tingle released from my plum, and images of the mysterious stranger running his hands and lips all over my body invaded my mind. I could see him. I could hear him. From the soft yet steady beating of his heart to his quipped breathing. I could even taste his minty breath on my tongue. Taking another sip, I rolled my eyes to the back of my head and placed my glass back on the board. Lust had taken over me. With my hands now submerged in water, I felt my right thigh bouncing.

My little pussy was begging to be touched, fondled, and played with. I sucked on my bottom lip, twirling my tongue around my mouth. My eye started twitching and I just couldn't help myself. I forced my legs open, found the budding center of my clit, and flickered my middle finger across it rapidly. The sensation from the water and my finger gave me an out-of-body experience.

I motioned my left hand up to my areola then to my lips, and sucked on my finger. Saliva dripped down my index and middle finger and I transferred the warm wetness to my breasts. My nipples were beyond hard, standing erect. Both index and middle fingers of each hand were going to town on my pussy and nipple simultaneously. I whimpered. I licked my lips and I imagined just how good it would feel to have Mr. GQ sliding his tongue and dick in and out of my mouth, pussy, and asshole.

"Fuck this tight-ass pussy!" I mustered aloud, turning myself on. Although I hadn't had sex in a while, I knew this was some good good I had over here, and I knew just how to get myself off.

Images of him stepping closer and closer, grabbing me by my neck, palming my pussy and my ass simultaneously had me ready to nut.

"Yeah, baby. Make me feel good." I hummed softly, and a strong hiss of passion fell out my mouth.

My toes were curling, and throwing up gang signs underwater. My neck was cramping but I was right there. On the verge. Right there. Just a little bit more. My fingers were now cramping as both hands were moving a mile a second as I fought for my orgasm. Pressure began to swell, and I felt my pussy about to release until a pestering sound blared from my phone.

"Fuck!" I screamed. The annoying ringtone blew my shit completely and I lost the spot that I was flickering. One minute after several annoying rings, the phone began to ring again. Irritated, I leaned over the tub and grabbed my phone that sat on the wooden stool.

As soon as I picked it up, I saw that it was nobody other than Nika. I watched it ring for the final time before hanging up. *I'd talk to her later. After I bust this nut.* The phone rang again and it was her once more. I kissed my teeth hard and answered the FaceTime call.

"Ahh shit. That nigga must have fucked the breaks off of you. Your ass soaking in the whirlpool." She screeched, her voice loud and pitchy.

I rolled my eyes, tired of her aggravating ass already.

"Actually, we kept it PG. Well more like PG-13."

Sucking her teeth, Nika plastered her face so close to the phone, I saw up her nostrils.

"You sure are a boring bitch. How you have that fine ass man come to your rescue late at night, free of charge, and don't give him no pussy?"

"Because what he requested was that I cook for him in lingerie. Not that I cook for him and have sex with him."

"Stop being so fucking literal, Eva."

"Well stop being so fucking annoying, clocking what I do with my pussy." I sassed. Nika was always doing way too much.

"Someone needs to clock it because apparently your ass doesn't know what to do with it or who to give it to."

Nika's brash comment irritated me, but she was right. I never really picked the right men. My sneaky and devious ex was a testament to that. While he was my first serious relationship, and the only man I've ever really loved, once I found out how badly he deceived me, it made me question if I ever really knew what love was. There was one thing for sure, and two things for certain; I knew what lust was and how it felt and I knew that I couldn't settle for that anymore.

"Right now, I don't need to be giving it to anyone. I'm still healing after everything with Jared."

"Forgive me. Well actually I don't care if you forgive me, but it has been nearly three fucking years since you've been with Jared. Now I know what he did was terrible and it may take you a long time to trust another man like that but you have to try." Nika's eyes had softened and her bottom lip hung into a sympathetic pout. "And this new guy is a start!"

I inhaled a deep breath and exhaled. "A start for just another fuck buddy! And I'm tired of giving my body to these niggas just to feel empty after the fact." Now I was pouting and on the verge of tears. "Which is why celibacy has been working for me."

Nika was silent, blinking her eyes and raising her brows, which meant that she was thinking hard.

"I'm sorry to burst your bubble girl, but you're not practicing true celibacy. You're just abstinent and holding onto that kitty kat." Holding her hands up in surrender, she bounced her shoulder and twisted her lip. "By all means you have every right to hold on to your honeypot, but how can you truly test your strength in celibacy if you don't even date, or at least date someone that you like?"

Nika shook her head and her bulging eyes shifted from side to side. "It's easy to be celibate or abstinent when you're not dating or even interacting with men. The true test is can you abstain from sex when you're dating or talking to a fine-ass man like Mr. Gideon Duke?"

Nika chuckled softly, rubbing her hands together like Birdman from Cash Money. "Exactly. Your ass doesn't stand a chance. So it's best you stop lying to yourself about this celibacy bullshit, and take your control back in this dating world."

I fumed, rolling my eyes as I listened to Nika attempt to lecture me. If it was anyone other than Nika I wouldn't dare take their advice on dating, but Nika had no problem getting a man, or taking someone else's man and keeping him. On her second engagement after her high school sweetheart and first husband passed away, Nika was qualified to talk.

"What exactly does that even mean, Nika?" I asked puzzled. I thought taking sex off the table meant that I was taking my control back, but clearly, I was wrong.

"Eva, you're sexy and the kind of work that you do is quite salacious. Yes, a lot of men will sexualize and objectify you. But men sexualize and objectify all women they find sexy or attractive, regardless of their job title. It's your job to stand in your sexiness and command your respect. Don't shy away from your sexiness, but understand that you can use it to get what you want. You just have to play your cards right, and if you want that man, you gotta go get him."

"But—"

"But nothing. Just remember, you can dangle the pussy without giving it away, and during this time, just be your loveable self and he will fall in love with you. Simple!"

I exhaled and leaned back into the tub of water when a text from an unsaved number popped up on my phone. I clicked on it, stumbling to my messages and it read like this:

My apologies for behaving like a madman. You're just breathtakingly sexy. Hopefully, I didn't turn you off completely, because I'd really like to see you again, this week perhaps. Let's meet at Centennial Park. I have tickets for the Sky View and we can do dinner after.

I returned back to the FaceTime call with a giddy smile and it did not go unnoticed.

"Uhh who the hell was that?"

"Gideon!" I squealed.

Nika's cheekbones rose as she stuck her tongue out. "Yessss! Saying what?"

Showing all thirty-two of my pearly whites, a smile truly from ear to ear, I filled her in. "He wants to take me on a date to Centennial Park to ride the Sky View and have dinner!"

"See bitch! He's feeling your ass!"

"Or the fact that I didn't give up the pussy and now he's on the hunt for it."

"Girl, are you slow? That man has seen you in lingerie, and from your reveal of PG-13, I'm sure he had his hands all in your pussy. To ask you on an intimate date like that just for some pussy that he's already soft-sampled makes no sense. He's intrigued by you, and it's not just because he wants to fuck! See this why your ass needs to be dating. You can't even pick up on the signs when a nigga likes you!" Nika sassed.

I titled my head and nodded. "I guess you're right!"

"Bitch, I am right! Now text that man back and confirm the date."

"I'll text back later. Don't want to seem too thirsty!"

Nika cut her eyes at me and pursed her lips. "Playing games.

See, that's exactly why your ass is single. Anyhow, I'm off this. I really just called to make sure he didn't kidnap your ass or anything. Romantic fairytale and all, these niggas do be crazy."

"Where you running off to that you're rushing me off the phone?"

Nika sucked her teeth. "If you must know, I've got lunch with Tyson later. Gotta stop by European Wax Center for a Brazilian."

"Oh ok. Enjoy babe."

"Oh, I will. And you don't forget to text that man back. I know how forgetful you can be."

Allowing a soft fume to roll off my tongue, I poked my lips forward. "Alright Nika, I'll text back to confirm."

"Good!"

seven

PRESSURE

GQ

Two days had gone by and still no text or confirmation back from Eva. I knew she saw my text because she had the audacity to leave her read receipts on. Part of me wanted to call her, but I was afraid she wouldn't answer and I didn't want to face that kind of rejection. Cinematic movies of her walking down the steps and her ass giggling, twirling on a pole, and dropping down into a split filled my mind.

Images of her Hershey kissed skin, her suckled juicy lips, her meaty thighs, and those seductive eyes were imprinted in my mind. Having watched her for years online, from her webcam days, to her early OnlyFans content, I was hooked. If not everyday, I watched her every other day. Most mornings I'd wake up, stretch out for my phone and mosy over to her Instagram or TikTok page, especially if I woke with a stiff cock. Sometimes I didn't even need to watch any of her explicit content. Just seeing her dressed in a bra and leggings turned me on, as she strutted in front of the camera, sashaying her hips and smacking her lips. Just the motion of her tongue as she talked was enough for me to jack off and bust a nice early nut. Whether she was twirling on the strip pole, working out with her trainer, or modeling and promoting undergarments and lingerie, watching Eva always satisfied my hunger.

Eva was truly my fantasy. Meeting her felt like a dream. Getting to know her was even more exciting. While I was undoubtedly sexually attracted to her, I was also intrigued. I wanted to know more about her upbringing, her dreams and aspirations beyond social media. I wanted to pick her brain, find out what she really thought about the worldly issues she addressed from time to time on her Tik Tok. I wanted to know if the caring, intellectual side of her was just a facade to seem woke or conscious or did she really care about the lack of running water in underdeveloped countries.

"Daddy! I'm going to the movies tomorrow with Tia and Tamera. Can I get some money?"

Gianna, my fifteen-year-old daughter startled me as she walked into the kitchen, her head down and eyes glued to her cell phone.

"Can you at least look at me, while you're begging?"

Her gaze shifted from her phone to me as she folded her arms. "Daddyyyy. Come on!"

"How much do you need?"

"Two hundred and fifty dollars."

I had to do a double-take to get a good look at my daughter. Gianna was exceptionally tall for her age, and since getting older she was becoming less lanky, as she started to fill out more. Now my baby girl had curves and was growing by the second.

Searching her face, I saw nothing but her mother. She had an angelic, smooth butterscotch-toned face just like her mom and I was doing everything I could to ensure she didn't turn out like her.

"What? Why do you need that much money to go to the movies?" I questioned. I made sure to close my laptop to give her my undivided attention. I would get back to the emails and invoices I had open in a bit.

Bouncing her knee and biting at her fingertips, she cleared her throat. "I wouldn't need that much if I had a car already. But since I don't, I need Uber money to get back and forth and spending money of course."

I pulled my top lip into the bottom one and placed my chin atop my fist. "Doesn't Tia and Tamera have cars?"

"Yes, but I don't want to ride with them."

"And why is that? If you girls are going to the same place, why not just offer to pay for gas and ride with them?"

Gianna's face turned as white as duppy as she twisted and fidgeted with her arms.

"Why don't you want to ride with them?" I questioned again.

"Uhh, I just want to make sure I get there and back safely."

My brows rose. "The twins are seventeen and they've been driving for a while, with a license and no car accidents. What's the issue?"

"Nothing Daddy!"

I stood from the bench attached to the kitchen island table and motioned closer to her. "You've never been good at lying and you know I always know when something is up. Talk to me, what's going on?"

Gianna blew out an agitated breath. "It's just sometimes Tia drinks too much."

I held my head to the ceiling. Great! Not that it was uncommon for teenagers to drink, but drinking and driving wasn't safe. These kids didn't grow up how my cousins and I did back in Guyana, drinking and driving. Besides, drinking and driving is legal in Guyana. In America, it's illegal and highly dangerous.

Passing her one of the debit cards from my wallet, I exhaled. "I'll text you the code. Do not spend more than two hundred and fifty dollars. I know Ubers are expensive but it shouldn't cost you more than one hundred dollars round trip and you shouldn't spend more than eighty dollars tops at the movies and for food. Try to come back with at least seventy dollars."

I tried my best to advise her to be a good steward of her money, well my money. The truth was that I needed her to understand the value of a dollar. Just because I had money didn't mean I was going to spoil her rotten or let her abuse me.

"Okay, Daddy. And thanks for not getting on me about Tia and Tamera's drinking. Trust me when I say I hate the smell and taste of liquor."

I looked into my baby girl's eyes and felt sincerity. While I didn't know if she was telling the truth, I wanted her to know that she didn't have to lie to me.

"Gianna, you're fifteen. Teenagers drink. I understand that. I'm just happy that you're concerned about your safety. And another thing, I don't want you to think that you have to lie to me or put on some kind of facade. If you don't like to drink, that's cool. But if you want to drink, make sure to buy and handle your own liquor. Don't allow anyone to pour you a drink and take your drink wherever you go. If you happen to leave it somewhere, just get another drink. And most importantly, if you ever find yourself out of it, or stranded, call me. Never be scared

46

to call me. I don't care what it is. I will drop everything to come to your rescue."

Gianna's eyes lit up and she rushed me with happiness. Wrapping her arms around me, she squeezed me tight and I squeezed her back. "Thanks, Daddy. I love you."

"I love you too baby girl. And you just reminded me that I have a date tomorrow too."

Gianna broke away from me and scratched her elbow nervously. "A date? Who are you dating, Daddy?"

I snickered, shaking my head as I watched my baby girl squirm in jealousy. "Don't question me, gal. Do I be all up in yuh business about every likkle bwoy that texts yuh phone? Nuh, so don't mind mi business, yuh hear?"

Gianna sucked her teeth and chuckled. "Gwan outta mi face, likkle gal." I chided.

Gianna scurried out of the kitchen and I returned to the island, opened my laptop then picked up my phone. Staring at the last text message I sent Eva, I grew irritable. I just had to see her and I wasn't about to double text her or call her multiple times. Fuck it, I knew where the fuck she lived. I was just gon have to pull up because there was just no way, I was taking no for an answer.

The very next day, I went to some fancy floral shop and picked up five dozen hot pink roses. I didn't want to get some basic red roses, so I had to step it up a notch. Hot pink roses were intended to make a statement and I needed Eva to hear me loud and clear. I wanted her sexy, chocolate-fluffy self. I even picked up a card and wrote a corny message in it. I realized that I was probably a bit too aggressive with her, which was why she hadn't returned my text. She probably thought I was a typical nigga just trying to get into her panties. Truthfully, she wasn't wrong. I did want to make love to her body in ways she had never felt before, but I also wanted to caress and soothe her mind and shower her with love and affection.

So, as I pulled up to her house, I took a deep breath, because I knew I had some bargaining to do, and I was ready, even if I had to fight with her to go out with me. I just needed a few hours to talk and get to know her better. I missed having that level of intimacy with a woman. It had been years since I felt safe talking to a woman. Part of me was hoping that Eva could change that.

After fixing my shirt and shaking my locs to make sure they weren't draping in my face, I finally felt ready. I pressed her doorbell, and a few seconds later, she appeared on the camera.

"Who is it?" She asked not looking directly at the camera and seeming to be quite occupied.

As she lifted her heart-shaped face, her voluptuous lips turned into a snarl, when she noticed it was me. "What do you want?"

"To take you out. I know you saw my text!" I asserted as I held the bouquet of roses higher in the camera for her to see.

"And if I didn't respond, what would make you bring your ass all the way to my home thinking that I'd change my mind?"

"Come on girl open up. At least come accept these roses I spent four hundred dollars on." I said as I held the large bouquet of roses in the camera.

A quick blush rose to her cheeks as she bit her lip. "Those are pretty," she mustered.

"Well come and get them. They're yours!"

"I don't know who you think you are but just because you got me some flowers, doesn't mean—"

"Gal, hush and come get the damn roses, already." As much as I was trying, this nice guy shit wasn't working. Eva needed a little aggression, and I was glad to give it to her.

She disappeared from the ring camera and within three minutes, she arrived at the door. Dressed in beige-colored leggings and a matching crop shirt, she looked relaxed. Her breasts were sitting high and her cinched waist atop her meaty thighs made a simple outfit look sexy on her. Her hair was shoulder length and bouncy and she had her toes out, with a crisp white paint job. Not too much, but just enough to make a nigga come home eagerly every night.

"Damn you so pretty!" I said, complimenting her as I handed her the roses.

She twisted her lip, rendering my compliment as bullshit, and blinked dramatically. "Thanks. And thank you for the flowers."

"You're welcome. Now get dressed. Our reservations are an hour away..."

"Who said I was going anywhere with you?" She argued, trying to balance that heavy ass bouquet in her hands.

"I did. Now hurry the fuck up and get dressed. I'll be waiting in the car for you."

She stood there, stunned without saying a word.

"And put on that perfume you had on the other night. It drove me crazy!"

Sighing with duck lips protruding from her mouth, she shook her head. "I bet."

eight
ROSES

EVA

I was definitely playing hard to get because the truth was GQ was turning me all the way on. The fact that he didn't double text me or even call, yet showed up at my house with flowers, had me looking at him differently. He was finally showing me another side to him, which affirmed exactly what Nika had said. He was interested in me. As we rode down I-285, we listened to soft R&B which consisted of Mary J Blige, Mariah Carey, and some of the super groups of the 90s; SWV, Total, and Jodeci.

"Turn that up, that's my song!" I patted his leg, as the sounds of Groove Theory's Tell Me blared through the speakers. The bass dropped and I sang along with every melody. Looking over at GQ, I saw him humming too.

"What you know about this? You was listening to R&B in Guyana?" I asked.

GQ sucked his teeth. "You crazy gal? Of course, I does listen to R&B growing up. What kind of question is that?" I loved how eloquently he switched between his West Indian and American accent.

I leaned back in my seat, jerking my neck and bulging my eyes. "Well excuse me. How would I know?"

"You grew up in Queens right?"

"South Ozone Park to be exact!"

GQ kissed his teeth and sighed as I watched him handle the steering wheel with one hand. His seat was leaned back as he sat up erect. His arms were so strong they were popping out of his thick leather jacket. Just taking in all of his features on top of the soothing cologne he wore turned me on even more.

"If you grew up in South Ozone Park, which is Little Guyana, you should know!"

"Well, to be honest, my neighbors played nothing but soca, reggae, dancehall, and Indian music. I never heard R&B or Rap and they had many barbecues and cookouts."

He glanced over at me quickly and pursed his lips. "Interesting. But just for your information, it's called Chutney Soca."

"Huh?"

"It's not Indian music. It's called Chutney Soca. Inspired by Indian, African, and soca fusions all mixed in one."

"Well, excuse me. I got it now!"

"You're excused… again."

I snickered as I rolled my eyes and turned my head to face the window. A few seconds later, I felt his warm hand on my thigh. I turned to face him and he clicked his tongue.

"Yuh tink yuh di only one wid a spice mouth? Trust me gal, yuh nuh wan fuh test mi."

His accent was so damn sexy, and the way he handled me, was every sexier. I didn't know what to say or do. All I knew was that this man was about to give me a run for my money, and I wasn't sure I was quite prepared.

We pulled up to Sky View and made our way through the crowd. I couldn't help but admire his swag. Seeing him again, made me realize just how tall he was. It was obvious that he worked out from how broad his shoulders were and the sway in his hips as he walked slightly ahead of me producing a commanding bop that just made me feel so protected.

Approaching the counter, GQ grabbed me by the hand, as he pulled out his phone. A black girl around my age's eyes lit up as GQ raised his head with his dreadlocks swinging in his face.

"Reservations for two," he said as he squeezed my hand tighter and showed her the phone with his other hand.

The worker scanned his phone, then shifted her gaze to me and twisted up her lip before poking them out and folding her arms. She looked me up and down then returned her attention back to GQ.

"What time do you want to ride? You can choose the next ride which starts in 15 minutes or you can choose a later time."

"Di next ride."

"Perfect. Let me get your wristbands." The whole time she spoke, she either avoided my gaze and focused all of her attention on GQ or was rolling her neck and cutting her eyes at me. I knew the nigga was fine, but damn. Couldn't she see that we were together? Her attitude was on ten, through the roof.

She pulled out a wristband and began to wrap it around GQ's hand. Then she chuckled and said "FYI, there's a weight limit of six hundred pounds. Handsome, you look like a solid 220, yourself."

Oh no the fuck she didn't. The last time I weighed myself, I was two hundred and eighty pounds. I know this bitch did not try to insinuate that I was almost four hundred pounds. Eva, keep your composure. Woosah, I thought.

"Don't worry about what my lady weighs. Just get her fucking wristband," GQ said, as he let go of my hand, raising his chin in the air. The crunchy sound of him cracking his knuckles was so profound, it blocked out all outside noise.

Ms. Attitude was on the rather chubby side too, but happened to be taller than me which distributed her weight a bit more evenly nonetheless she was still on the fluffy side. She rolled her eyes and ripped the wristband off the sheet of paper. "Damn, you didn't have to curse me out," she mustered as she wrapped the band around my wrist.

"And you didn't have to get smart with me and my lady."

A smirk crept up my mouth, as I watched the girl's face go slack. Just when I thought I was going to have to get ignorant, GQ stepped up and handled it.

"Alright you got it, relax." She huffed and puffed dramatically. "Follow the signs towards the back. Enjoy your ride!"

GQ grabbed me by the hand and motioned me forward, before saying "Enjoy the rest of your long ass shift and your likkle ten dollars an hour," he added before snickering.

"Bitch think she's somebody with her bullshit ass job. Go fix that nasty ass wig before talking about someone's weight!"

"All right, Gideon. Come on. It's all right." I ordered him, as I pulled him away.

"Nah, fuck that, she was out of line."

Just seeing him angry and all up in arms about me was another turn-on. The fact that he jumped to my defense immediately without me having to say anything showed me how much of a protector he really was.

"Thanks for standing up for me," I said as we stood in front of the V.I.P. gondola.

GQ pulled me close, and I was now submerged in his scent as he hugged me, my face lying on his stomach. He was wearing a thick leather jacket, crisp white Tee, and some designer sneakers that had large colorful shoelaces through them. I didn't know the name of the brand, but I had seen a lot of rappers wear them.

"Of course, babe. I wasn't about to let that bitch play with you. Nah, not at all."

He grabbed me tighter, then leaned down and kissed me. His lips roamed mine as his hands traveled up and down my skirt, tenderly caressing my thighs. He was feeling me up from the inside of my thighs the wool on the forearm of my coat. His touch and embrace warmed me up from the windy chill. It felt so good being in his arms.

A few minutes later, the white male worker, opened the door to the gondola. The first thing I noticed when I stepped inside was a bouquet of pink carnations sitting on the red and black leather seats. There was also a red box of chocolates next to it and a bottle of Moscato. Covering my mouth with my hands, I was in complete awe.

"Good looks man," GQ said to the white male worker and passed him two hundred dollars.

"No problem boss. Everything else you requested is in the middle compartment," the worker said.

The two men dapped each other up and GQ joined me inside the gondola. Once the door was shut, GQ grabbed me by the wrist, pulling me into his embrace. He sat down and I followed, sitting on his lap with the bouquet in my hands.

"Flowers again?"

"Of course. Do you like them?" He asked.

"I love them!" I blushed.

GQ removed the flowers from my hands and placed them on the chair next to him. He grabbed the box of chocolates and opened it. He then pulled out a heart-shaped small chocolate and held it to my mouth. Looking into his eyes, there was so much intensity between us. He batted his lashes, signaling for me to relax. I opened my mouth and he popped the chocolate into it. The flavors of raspberry cream hit my taste buds immediately.

I sucked in my bottom lip, savoring the taste.

"That was good. You're quite the romantic, Mr. GQ."

"Nah, I just realized that we didn't really get off on the right foot. And I wanted to show you who I really am," he confessed.

I licked my lips and lowered my eyes. "So, this is who you are? A lover boy?"

He chuckled. "Something like that," he answered, then kissed me passionately.

After a full-blown make-out session, I pushed him back. He had my nipples hard, and my pussy throbbing. This was not my idea of a first date, at all. I shimmied out of his lap and peered out the glass window, taking in the scenery of Atlanta at large. The sky was a baby blue hue and the clouds were light and airy. Atlanta was a charming city that I grew to love and to think all these years I've been here, I've never been to a carnival or on a Ferris wheel.

"Here, babe." GQ's touch startled me.

I turned and he passed me a glass of Moscato. I grabbed it from him and took a sip.

"So, I'm your babe already?" I asked inquisitively.

"Yeah. That's a problem?"

"Uh, you don't think we're moving too fast?"

GQ's pinched expression and the narrowing of his eyes told me he was annoyed by my question.

"No, I don't. I feel like I've known you forever," he said. And that's when it hit me, he had to be a fan. He had to have seen me on IG or subscribed to my OnlyFans or something to feel like he'd known me forever after our brief, steamy encounters.

"Well, I don't feel the same. Besides the bio on your website, I don't really know you at all."

GQ raised his brows and crossed his arms. "What do you wanna know?"

"Everything. But first, I'd like to know how long you've been subscribed to my OnlyFans?"

GQ stopped tapping his foot, his facial muscles went slack as he stared at me with a flat gaze. "Since you've started it. About five years now." He admitted.

My eyes bulged. He was an OG fan if he subscribed to my Only Fans back in 2018. New to the platform, I struggled to even make one thousand dollars a month the first year of my OnlyFans career. Now I was bringing in one hundred thousand dollars a month from OnlyFans. Before he could be fronting, just trying to impress me. I needed to test his knowledge. Make sure he knew his shit.

"So if you're an OG Fan, what was my very first name on Only Fans?"

"Eva With The Good Cat!" He blurted out immediately.

I busted out into a laugh, shaking my head. "Oh my God. You really are a super fan. Only my day one supporters know that I went by that."

"And only your day one supporters know why you changed the name too." He interjected.

I poked my lips out then grinned, and rolled my eyes flirtatiously. "And why is That?" I challenged him.

"Once Sukihana blew up and went viral with Suki With The Good Coochie, you wanted to separate yourself from her brand, even though you coined the term first."

Mouth wide, I leaned back from him and folded my arms. "Wow. You remembered that video? I deleted it not even an hour after I posted it. That was four years ago."

"I know." He declared with a sense of surety. "I told you I've been a fan."

"I see. So let me ask you this, since we're adults and we're being honest. Are you truly interested in getting to know me, or do you just want to fuck me?"

Without hesitation, he blinked slowly. "Both."

At the sound of his response, I scooched away from him, creating more distance between us. I knew he wasn't truly interested in me. He was just an obsessed fan. Thank God, I went with my gut and didn't fuck him.

He scooched closer to me and planted a kiss on my shoulder. "But just because I want to fuck you, doesn't mean I'm not open to loving you."

I sucked my teeth. At this point, I was convinced that he would say any fucking thing to get his way.

"You can't love someone you don't know. So tell me this. What happened in your last relationship?"

He sighed and for the first time since I'd met him backed away from me.

"It's a long story."

Bucking my eyes and jerking my neck, I laid the attitude on thick. "We're in the air for a while. We've got nothing but time."

GQ exhaled and I could see the irritation on his face. "She left me and her daughter and never came back. I found out two years ago that she lives in California with her husband and her three kids."

GQ's entire posture had changed. Between the caved chest, slumped shoulders and him staring down at his empty hands, I knew it was a lot for him to reveal that. I grabbed his hand and squeezed it.

"Damn, babe. I'm so sorry to hear that," I said sympathetically.

"It's cool. So I'm your babe, now?" He chuckled, lightening the mood.

I shoved him playfully and snickered. "I see what you did there."

"Look gyal, my motto has always been the same: when you see a woman you want, go and get her. No if, ands, or buts." GQ lifted my chin for me to face him, peering directly into his eyes.

"Even if she has an OnlyFans," I asked, my vulnerability seeping through.

"Especially if she has an OnlyFans," he responded and grabbed me by my neck and kissed me roughly.

I don't know what took over me, but I couldn't resist him. I jumped on top of him, straddling him with my thunder thighs, and pulled his jacket then his shirt off. I kissed all over his chest, trailing my tender lips up and down his washboard abs. His grunts increased, and his grips on my ass became rougher. His touch was just doing something to me that I couldn't control. I wanted him and I wanted him now. My commitment to celibacy couldn't save me at this moment. I needed him.

As I wrestled with confliction, I continued gnawing at his body, sucking on his abs until I tasted his sweat. In a quickness, the roles were now reversed, and he was on top of me, fondling my breasts and rubbing in between my thighs. For a second, he broke away from me. A screech alerted me to him opening the storage compartment hoisted inside the gondola. He reappeared with a pink rose toy and a devilish smile as he licked his lips. He pressed down on the center of the rose toy and the loud vibration excited us both.

We shared a smile.

"It's so damn hard not to overly sexualize you, especially as an admirer. Look at you, you're edible in every way. But I am kind of happy you're celibate, because it forces us to take things slower, than I,--- then we, usually would." He stuttered on the last part of the sentence. "So, out of respect for your celibacy, I won't try to persuade you to fuck me. But that doesn't mean, I can't please you."

Before I knew it, GQ placed the bud of the rose on my clit, and the sensation ran through my body like a bolt of lightning. Quick, fast, and intense. I placed one hand on the shoulder of the seat as I struggled to keep my composure. A warm wetness replaced the sharp vibration and that's when I noticed GQ's head was in between my thighs. Licking, sucking, and slurping me up. One hand on his head, and the other on the seat, I clenched my thighs together as I moaned softly.

"Yes. Oh my God. It feels so good," I whispered.

GQ pried my legs open further and stuck his tongue in and out of my opening, shifting from my honeypot to my clit. My legs started shaking, and my hands were bracing his shoulders, until he hopped up from the laying position, forcing me into a pretzel and sucking viciously on my clit as he entered two fingers into me. He then placed the rose back on my clit as he pulsed his two fingers in and out of me.

"FUCKKKKKK!" I screamed, shaking my legs uncontrollably, as water shot out of my pussy.

GQ looked up at me with a smirk and bit his lip before sucking up all of my juices. I could feel my clit pulsating in his mouth. When I had finally stopped cumming, he chuckled and said "Damn, she's a squirter."

MY LADY

GQ

For the next few days, I just couldn't get her out of my mind. We were texting and Face Timing daily nonstop, learning more and more about each other's interests, dislikes, and experiences. From our childhood, to pop culture, we were covering new territory every day and I was enjoying it. And to think we were getting so close and I was feeling her and we hadn't even had sex yet. Sure I sucked the nut out of her, but I never entered her, and I was fine with that.

Just getting to know her was enough for me. It also felt good to not have to hide the fact that I was subscribed to her Only Fans. I didn't have to feel like a creepy fan. I could admire her openly. On top of that, it was nice to hear about all of her plans and endorsements she had going on. While, it was obvious that she had transitioned out of creating sexual content, learning that she had fashion and beauty endorsements lined up impressed me.

She was already a big deal and more than just an Instagram Hoe in my mind, but now I was proud to talk about her with my guys, without fear of being judged.

I tapped my foot impatiently, as I waited for my boys Twan and Ice to pull up. I was at our favorite bar spot in Buckhead where we met two to three times a month. App surfing on my phone, I couldn't stop myself from drooling over Eva. I would switch back and forth from her Instagram to her Only Fans and fantasize about what I was going to do to her when we finally crossed that bridge. Truthfully, the fact that she was celibate didn't really bother me, especially because she was mentally stimulating me.

First off, she was a great listener, and she asked thought-provoking questions that showed me she was really interested in me. She wasn't just infatuated with my dark skin, long dreadlocks, and muscular build like most women I dated were. It was refreshing to talk to a woman who was a true conversationalist. I yawned dramatically and covered my mouth. I was running on three hours of sleep, having stayed on the phone with Eva all night. We spent a total of nine hours on the phone playing 21 questions, Never Have I Ever and just laughing and getting to know each other.

As the bartender placed another beer down in front of me, I spotted Ice and Twan approaching the bar.

"What's good boss?" Twan greeted me. I stood and returned his dap.

"It's about time ya'll niggas pulled up," I joked, as I exchanged grips with Ice.

"Man, you already know how that Atlanta traffic is on the 285," Ice explained.

"Yeah, yeah, yeah whatever nigga," I replied. "First round is on me. What y'all niggas want? This is crucial. I think I found the one!"

Ice, who I've been friends with since we met back in trade school seventeen years ago, shook his head. "This nigga!" he exclaimed, turning to Twan and twisting his lip.

Twan was a work friend, who started out as Ice's electrical assistant and bounced back and forth between both Twan and I's companies. Since he was five years younger, he didn't have as many years of experience as us, but having trained under both of us, he soaked up tons of knowledge. So much to the point that he had secured three major contracts; one with the City of Atlanta, the second with the Doubletree Hilton, and the final one with Grady Hospital. He now was providing Ice and me with work.

"We gotta hear bruh out, Ice. I ain't never hear G talk like this." Twan added.

He wasn't lying. He hadn't been around when Gianna's mom and I were together. Ice remembered how in love I was with her. Ice remembers how it tore me up when she not only left me but also left her daughter. Ice also witnessed how the betrayal, sneaky and devious bullshit she pulled changed me, and turned me into the heartless, distant, detached bachelor that Ice and Twan knew me to be.

"Shit, me either. It's been years, I've never seen my man smile this wide. Who is she?" Ice laughed. "Nigga skin glowing, cheeks looking all rosy." Ice continued laughing. Twan joined in and they exchanged brotherly dabs.

"Fuck you, nigga." I said.

They settled into the bar seats, and Ice rested his arms on the island. Twan waved the bartender over and ordered three Guinness.

"But seriously, who is she?" Ice pressed.

While I was still reluctant to tell them about Eva, I was full of warm, gushy excitement and I just needed to share it with my guys. Eva truly had me at a loss for words, that I didn't even know how to say. I just unlocked my phone, pulled up her Instagram, and passed Ice the phone.

Ice sucked his teeth dramatically. "This is this Instagram, Only Fans bitch you've been obsessing over. Stop playing, nigga."

Immediately I got defensive. "She's not a bitch. Her name is Eva. And I'm serious nigga. I'm feeling her."

Twan grabbed the phone from Ice zoomed in on her picture, and shook his head slowly.

"You and the rest of them sucker ass niggas on IG that's impressed by a half-naked bitch selling her ass." Ice hackled.

The Irish bartender placed the three Guinness on the island and Twan was the first to pick his up and jugged down a gulp.

"Watch ya mouth, nigga, talking about my lady." I bucked, clearing my throat and cracking my knuckles.

Ice broke out into a haughty, exaggerated laugh. "Relax, nigga. You about to beat my ass over a bitch you don't even know? You're more than obsessed. We need to get your ass some help. You might really be a sex addict. You're not only making this bitch richer by subscribing to her Only Fans and giving her your hard-earned money, but now you're obsessing about being with her, knowing you ain't never gon' meet that bitch a day in your life. This shit can't be real." Ice laughed again, then picked up his beer.

"Nigga, I met her almost two weeks ago, and I'm feeling her."

"Oh shit. Word, my boy?" Twan inquired. "How many followers she got on IG again?"

Ice picked up my phone, scanning its screen for confirmation. "Ten million."

"Damn, she's kind of a big deal," Twan, said.

Ice chuckled again and bounced his shoulders. "Not you too, impressed by another hoe showing her ass online."

Twan snatched the phone out of Ice's hand and scrolled down continuously, as his gaze narrowed in on the screen.

"Nah, bruh she ain't no Instagram hoe. She's actually a pole fitness instructor and influencer. Looks like she just teamed up with L.A. Fitness to do a thirteen-city tour, bringing pole fitness to their branches, before fully launching an exclusive online pole fitness program on their website. That's big, Ice."

Slapping the air, Ice sighed. "Once, a hoe always a hoe."

"Not true," Twan laughed, playing devil's advocate.

"Nigga stop calling her a hoe. Like, I said I'm feeling her. I know it hasn't been long but she's giving me a feeling I haven't felt in a long time. Like on a mental note, you know."

Ice grunted several times until it evolved into a condescending laugh. "Right. Nigga, if the pussy is immaculate, just say that. You don't gotta front for us, especially not me."

"Nah, I didn't even fuck yet. She's actually celibate. I just really fuck with her vibe. Our conversations, how she listens to me without judging. You know, shit like that."

Ice turned his chair slightly to the side looking directly at T'wan. "This nigga bugging. How you let a sex worker tell you she's celibate and you actually believe that shit? Yeah, you simping for real."

Part of me didn't want to tell them the truth, that I actually tasted her, because I didn't want to hear how she was a liar and a hoe when the truth was that the vibe between us was undeniable, which led to her allowing me to taste her sweetness. I didn't want to hear any more doubt about Eva, so I kept that knowledge to myself. They already thought I was a simp for subscribing to her OnlyFans. It didn't hurt for them to call me a simp, but hearing how Ice was talking about Eva had me on edge.

"Look I don't care what either of you niggas got to say. I'm fucking with her and that's that. And I'm gon tell you this last time, stop referring to my lady as a hoe!"

"Your lady? Nigga, you ain't even get your dick wet yet, but she's your lady? Once a hoe lover, always a hoe lover. I thought you gave up on hoes after Gina left."

The one thing I hated about Ice was how quick he was to throw things up in my face. He thought because he married his high school sweetheart, who lost her virginity to him and has only been with him, that all other women were hoes. He thought that a woman who dressed provocatively was the bottom of the bottom and should be treated as dirt.

"Nah nigga, you foul for even bringing that up. Just because I'm secure enough to date bad bitches, doesn't mean they're all hoes or that I'm a hoe lover."

Ice picked up his beer and took a swig. "Okay, okay. Maybe they're not all hoes, but this BBW one, she's a straight 304, selling her body on the World Wide Web. Gina was just a local stripper. Either way, you've got a type my boy, and it's definitely NOT wifey material."

"Fuck you, nigga. Just because you married a bitch that can't suck dick and has no sex appeal whatsoever, doesn't mean you know wifey material. Shit, the bitch had no choice but to marry you, she got pregnant at seventeen years old. You wanna talk about simp. Only niggas that marry a bitch just because she got pregnant are simps. Go touch some grass nigga. You ain't never had in your miserable life have a bitch as bad as Gina or Eva." I bucked.

"C'mon bruh, don't hit below the belt, talking about dawg ole lady now," T'wan intervened.

"Nah fuck that, he running his mouth about my baby momma and my new lady. Fuck him."

Ice chuckled and placed his beer on the table. "Baby momma and hoe ain't never been comparable to wife, so watch your fucking mouth talking about mine."

"And remember the same when it comes to Gina or Eva."

"Now, Gina I understand. She was a bad bitch, and still is. Fine, tall, slim thick, and light-skinned with hair down her back. What I don't get is your obsession with this fat, sloppy chick. I mean, I get wanting to have fun with that, but taking her seriously, what the fuck is wrong with you, bruh?"

Anger rolled from the lining of my stomach to my vocal cords.

"You're so fucking shallow, you can't fathom that beauty isn't exclusive to slim and light-skinned. Taking Gina seriously was probably the worst thing I ever fucking did. First off, Gina was never my type, because I've always been into BBWs and you know that. Gina was selfish and messy both physically and socially and she was a terrible listener. I just got caught up with the pussy, that monster head, and her cooking. I can't lie, for a skinny American bitch, she sure could throw down, but other than that, she wasn't the one. What kind of bitch leaves their daughter at two years old with the neighbor while I'm at work and hasn't called or visited since. Gianna is fifteen years old."

Ice got up from the bar stool and patted me on the shoulders. "I mean I get all that. But tons of fine-ass hoes listen, that isn't messy or selfish. Nigga, this is Atlanta. You don't have to settle for an out-of-shape, overweight IG model."

I knew he was trying to get a rise out of me, and it was working. Ice knew the situation with Gina was a sore spot for me, so to even bring that up was down low. Truthfully, I had buried all of my feelings for Gina, but being reminded of my failures in love or the fact that I chose her didn't make me feel good. Most importantly, the way he spoke about Eva infuriated me and made me want to knock both of his eyes out. In just a short period of time, I've gotten to know Eva beyond the physicality, it was evident that she was a smart businesswoman, established and disciplined. She was more than an IG model to me, and I just needed my friends to respect that.

"Respectfully, my lady may be overweight, but she's shapely as fuck and I'm feeling her, and I don't want to hear no slick or sly shit about her, and that's on everything nigga."

Ice sucked his teeth and shook his head back and forth. "Whatever you say, nigga. You like it, I love it."

MY MAN

EVA

"**M**akeup! Can we buff out Eva's cheekbones a bit more? They are too rosy. Let's soften it up a bit." The British photographer's heavy Saxon influence riddled all throughout his tone. A hint of playful sarcasm was also present but he kept me on point for the last three hours.

Today was my final photoshoot with Ashley Stewart for their annual pageant. The creative director requested that today's shoots would feature only evening gown looks. Being that the company was launching a full evening gown line, they wanted to feature me as their evening gown model. Cinched in an emerald green mermaid gown, and a blonde wig install styled into a flawless updo, I looked stunning. Most importantly, I felt beautiful.

The makeup artist, a young Hispanic girl buffed my face with her brush several times before spraying the setting spray all over me. She tilted her head side to side, looking at my face from every angle then smiled. "All good, mami!" Her Latin accent was thick and heavy, but her smile was inviting.

I smiled back, puckering my lips and getting ready for the camera. This was my fifth look, and we had to go through a full makeup change for this shot so I know the makeup artist was tired, but nonetheless, she was a great sport. Now that the eyes of the entire set were on me, it was time for action.

"Let's go!" The photographer shouted.

Doja Cat's "Agora Hills" played through the studio at a medium level.

I turned to the left, struck a pose, and softened my eyes. Click.

"Beautiful. Stay just like that. Raise your head, pull in your back, and pucker your lips."

I did as I was told, and he snapped away, gathering several photos.

"Sway, move. Do your thing."

I took his advice and got into full model mode. Moving my hands along my shoulder, onto my hips, and in front of me, I delivered countless poses for Ashley Stewart to feature on their website. Turning around, I allowed the photographer to get pictures of the back of the gown. The shutter sound from the camera ceased, and a loud sigh rang through the studio.

"That's a wrap!"

Claps from the production staff and the rest of the crew permeated the studio.

"You've got everything?" The creative director, a seasoned Asian woman shouted to the photographer.

"Yup! We're all good."

Relieved that the shoot was finally over, I wobbled towards the dressing room in the skin-tight gown that had me cinched in so tight that it felt like I was wearing a corset.

"Eva, someone is here to see you," one of the production assistants announced as he stepped in front of me.

I scrunched my face because who the hell was here to see me. Without saying a word, I followed him. Holding the bottom of my dress, I stepped over the white backdrop and made my way to the other side of the studio. As I crossed the threshold near the exit, I was surprised to see GQ standing there with a huge assortment of fruit from Edible Arrangements.

"Hey, beauty," he said greeting me with a big smile.

I returned his smile. "Thanks, Neil," I shouted to the production assistant who had already turned his back and started to walk away.

"You got it, Eva!" Neil shouted back.

As I returned my attention back to GQ, I noticed that he was also wearing a UPS uniform. With the milk chocolate-colored khakis and the matching brown polo, he looked good as fuck. His soft locs were hanging down, draping his face, and he had a cap over his head, that made his eyes appear really low, his mysterious appearance was turning me on in a dangerous way.

"What are you doing here?" I asked, utterly surprised.

A smile etched across his face. "Here to see my baby!" He exclaimed as he stepped closer to me, his hands still full with the assortment of fruit. "Damn you look - beautiful just isn't enough, baby. You look exquisite. Turn around for me, do a spin gyal," GQ said, complimenting me.

I did as I was told, and the kissing of his teeth persisted. "Ohhhh gosh," he hissed, his Guyanese accent really prominent. Moving the assortment of fruit to the side, he leaned in for a kiss,

71

and I caught it. Our lips petted each other as he drew me in with his tongue, pulling me closer in a tongue tug-of-war. After about a minute of kissing, we separated, both out of breath.

"Let me get out of this dress, baby. Give me a minute," I said, turning away.

His footsteps followed me, so I turned around and gazed at him. His eye widened and I assumed he raised his brow since his hat rode up a tad bit.

"Who's going to help you out of your dress if I let you go on alone?"

I licked my lips to hide the infectious grin that was swirling in my heart and a second away from overwhelming my face. I lowered my eyes, flickering them three times, and flirting with him like a teenage girl in heat. I latched onto his hand and guided him through the studio toward my dressing room. Eyes from the production staff followed us until we reached the threshold near my room. Once inside, the door slammed closed behind us, he set the fruit aside and swooped me into his arms.

He kissed me, rubbing the mesh of my dress as he fondled me. His strong hands traveled my body, as he nuzzled the bridge of his nose up and down my neck sending spurts of magic warmth that just felt heavenly, almost too good to be true. It had only been one month since GQ and I had been seeing each other, and we hadn't had sex yet, but the sexual chemistry between us was explosive. The romance was there, and I can't lie I was enjoying getting to know him without sex involved.

"Turn around," GQ instructed. "Let me help you."

The warmth of his hands brushed against my upper back, and sent chills down my spine, as he glided my zipper down, revealing my shapewear. He knelt all the way down allowing me to step out of the gown. Half naked, I felt confident and safe in his presence.

"Where does this go?"

"In this wardrobe bag," I mentioned as I shuffled towards the clothes rack and picked up a black garment bag attached to a velvet hanger. I zipped it down, and held it open, as GQ stuffed the dress inside it.

"Thank you for coming all the way down here, in that sexy uniform to drop off the fruit, babe. That was so sweet. But seriously what are you doing here? It's the middle of the day!"

"And? Did you forget I own my own business and have workers which means I control my schedule and theirs?"

I cut my eyes at him and twisted my lips.

"I'm a boss too, Ms. Eva."

"Oh really?" I said flirtatiously.

"Spend the day with me. I'm kid-free for the night and it's about time you inspect my apartment!"

"Inspect?" I raised my brows suspiciously.

"Yeah, I know how you women are. Gotta inspect a nigga crib to decide if he's boyfriend material or not! We might as well get it over with now, 'cause in my mind you're already mine."

I chuckled at his wittiness. Although funny, he was absolutely right. The last thing I'd want is for him to be a fine, dirty motherfucker so it was about time, I made a visit to his house.

As soon as we entered his home, a strong cinnamon aroma hit my nostrils, tantalizing my senses. There was a homely scent and feel to his place that was present from the purple bluish paint on the walls to the dim lights and the accentuation of natural light beaming through the windows.

"Welcome to my humble abode."

GQ had let go of my hand and walked about the living room, allowing me to watch his every move, from the sway of his back and the stride from his hips. He wasn't just oozing big dick energy, grown man energy was seeping from his pores.

"It smells good in here, babe" I complimented his taste in scents.

"There's this electric oil burner I use. It filters all through the house for hours."

"Ima need one of those."

"For sure, baby. I got you. Let me take your coat and show you around." GQ offered, like the gentleman he was.

I turned my back to him, dropped my shoulders and my wool coat slid off. He held my coat in one arm while pulling my hands into his as he led me through the house.

We passed by the kitchen which had an antique, yet lavish flair. Decked out with all the bells and whistles of the top-of-the-line antique kitchens, it was obvious that he modeled his kitchen after his mother's or perhaps his grandmother's kitchen.

An indigo-blue tin of shortbread cookies sat out on the island. I broke away from his tight hold and ran my fingers over the tin. "I haven't seen these cookies in years. My childhood is literally in that box of cookies."

GQ folded his arms and lowered his eyes. "You sure you're not West Indian?"

"Positive!"

"Hmm, I don't know! These cookies are a staple in every Caribbean household."

I opened the tin and grabbed three cookies, stuffing one in my mouth immediately. GQ shuffled towards the refrigerator and pulled out two small bottles.

"Apple or orange juice?"

"Apple juice, duh!"

He tossed the bottle of Dole juice toward me, I grabbed it, cracked it open, and took a long sip.

"Just like my daughter Gianna. She prefers apple juice over orange too. Come on, let me show you one of her rooms." His back straightened and his head lifted, his chin completely in the air. It was obvious that he took pride in being a father.

"One of her rooms? How many does she have?"

"Just three."

"Just three!" I mocked him. "She's a lucky girl."

"She is," he said sternly, without a chuckle or hint of laughter.

Pushing open the door to what looked like a modest bedroom from the outside, I was met by a full-on makeup studio. Bright lights illuminated the room as we walked in, highlighting three stations, all of which had the words "Gi'Gi GlamBox" spelled out in pink glowing lights.

"So I take it, GiGi's quite the little cosmetologist?"

"Yeah, she is. She does all of her friends' hair and makeup, and she's really good at it. I told her, that as soon as she turned eighteen if she wanted to enroll in cosmetology school, I'd be right there to support her."

Hearing how much GQ loved and supported his daughter warmed my heart, but also stung me in a place where I thought I had healed from. Seeing dads love on their daughters and adore them made my chin tremble, and feelings of inadequacy and worthlessness filled my heart. To conceal my negative thoughts from creeping on my face, I fought hard to push the lump back down my throat. Growing up without a father didn't bother me nearly as much when I was a child. Now being an adult and recognizing how important a father is in the life of a girl child especially, I felt empty and ashamed that I, like many other black girls grew up without a daddy. That's why it hurt me to the core, when…

"You okay, babe?" GQ's question brought me back to the center, which I was grateful for but instantly regretted. He was onto me. He could sense the change in my energy.

"Yeah, I'm good." I lied.

"You sure?"

I nodded quickly and switched the subject. "I bet she makes a lot of money. With this setup and all the best products she's got here, I know she does a good job."

"Yeah, she does. But I don't allow her to charge anyone, because she's not licensed and she's just a kid. I don't need her thinking she's grown just because she's making a little bit of money. She still gets an allowance for doing chores and she's had a few summer jobs to teach her the importance of a dollar, but I want my baby to focus on school, and having fun right now. If she is serious about making cosmetology a career and starting a business for herself, we will cross that bridge when we get there."

While, it stung a bit, hearing him talk so confidently and matter-of-fact about his daughter was still heartwarming. It was evident that he was proud of her, invested in her, and had her best interests at heart. This was my first time dating a single father, so dealing with a man who was as involved and active as he was, was new to me.

"Look at you. And the Daddy of the Year award goes to…"

"To me for sure! 24/7, 365 days in a year. I'm here through it all."

"That's a beautiful thing... I know she's happy to have you."

"Yeah, but it doesn't matter how much I do, it will never replace the hole in her heart from her mother abandoning her. That mother-daughter bond is important."

I nodded in agreement, searching his emotion-filled face. Never having a father had already fucked me up when it came to choosing the right men to date. I couldn't imagine not having Evette in my corner. She was the reason I turned out halfway decent. She was the reason I went on to college.

"Yeah, you're right about that. My mom and I are tight. She's not my best friend, but we're super close."

"What about your dad?"

I was hoping he hadn't asked. Now, really wasn't the time to get all sappy. I was enjoying our time together.

"I'd rather talk about him another time. I just want to enjoy the moment with you."

Without saying a word, GQ grabbed me closer, wrapping his arms around my neck. He kissed his teeth loudly and let out a sigh. "Ehh, I'll let it slide for now. I won't pressure you or nothing but there's gon come a time where you gon have to open up and show me all of you. Even the painful parts."

I lowered my head in submission. The last man I opened up to was Jared, and he used my vulnerabilities to manipulate, and victimize me. I may have been ready to open my legs to GQ, but I wasn't quite ready to let him in my heart or mind for that matter. I was at a loss for words.

"You hear me?" He wouldn't let up.

"Yes, I heard you. When I'm ready, we can talk about my

father and my ex, but right now, I'm enjoying just focusing on you, and us."

"Uh, huh. Okay." Stepping behind me, he placed his firm hands on my shoulders. He massaged his thumbs into my muscles.

"You're so tense." He whispered in my ear. Digging his thumbs deeper into my shoulders, a feeling of euphoria came over me so strongly that I felt my knees buckling. At that moment, nothing else mattered. Not my past, not my trauma, or my insecurities. All I wanted was Mr. Gideon Duke, real bad!

GREENLIGHT

GQ

Eva's body was truly a work of art and the perfect silhouette shadowed through my dimly lit massage room. Red rose petals covered the floor, the room set a glow with a dozen candles scattered about, and an aroma of minty eucalyptus filled the air. This was all a part of my plan and we were just getting started. Seeing her mouth drop open was priceless. No amount of money could buy that, only tender loving care, could.

With her fingers wrapped in mine, I led her through a puddle of rose petals.

"Babe, what is all of this? Oh my God."

"Everything you deserve!" I deepened my voice, enunciating clearly for her to hear me. She needed to know she was worth it.

She chuckled, turned back to me, and threw a sexy smirk my

way. She had so much confidence, in nothing but a G-string on. Bountiful, voluptuous curves draped her entire body, from her rolls, and her muffin top, down to her thunder thighs and ass. I don't care what anyone says. I don't care what any other man thinks, BBW women have the best bodies. Eva was perfect to me.

"You're so extra."

"Hush, hush, gal. Come lay on the table, face up," I instructed her as I let her hand go and smacked her on the ass.

She cooed like a naughty girl, causing my dick to harden. She had me hooked without even fucking her. Just the thought of fucking her was satisfying. But getting to know her, and exploring her was even more stimulating. I wanted to take my time with her, and I wanted to tap into other forms of intimacy that didn't involve actual penetration.

So I came prepared. With a rolling tray full of strawberries, cucumbers, caramel, and whipped cream, I was ready, willing, and able to explore every crevice of her body if allowed. I wanted to devour her, but really and truly, I wanted to savor her until the very last drop. I needed her tender for me, so I knew I had to slow-cook her, and I was enjoying every minute of it.

"Let's play a game."

"What kind of game?" She asked, lifting her neck up from the massage table, still looking at me from an upside-down position.

"21 Questions. But here are the rules. When you fall asleep and run out of questions to ask, I'm allowed to coat your entire body in chocolate and lick it off."

A deep laughter rolled from the pit of her stomach. "You're insane. You wanna la-la-la-lick me from my head to my toes."

She sang, following the melody of Ludacris' hit song "What's Your Fantasy."

Clapping my hands, I burst out in laughter. "What you? Ah comedian, gal?" I kept my accent to a minimum with Eva. Even though she was from New York and familiar with the culture, she was still a Yankee. But sooner or later, once we were official, she'd understand all mi patios and lingo. It was just a matter of time.

"Yeah. I'm known for making people laugh," she said. We both laughed at the sarcasm in her tone.

Rubbing oil onto my hand, I approached the table and massaged my palms on Eva's stomach. Stroking up and down to her chest, then back down her thigh, I applied medium pressure and consistent acupressure. I repeated this process on the left side of her body, then grabbed a strawberry from the tray and sprayed some whipped cream on it.

"I got the first question! But open up first." I instructed her

Eva opened her mouth and I fed her the strawberry. She sucked the whipped cream off the tip and bit into it. I removed my hand, allowing her to chew and swallow, and then I leaned over the table and planted a sensual kiss on her lips.

"What are you afraid of?" I asked, jumping right into the deep questions. I wasn't about to play with this girl. Before I thought about putting it on her, I needed to make sure she was sane, like for real.

"Dying alone." She said so curtly, that it hit me to the core. I could finally feel her being vulnerable and honest with me.

"I think that's everybody's fear. Both men and women. Not too many are brave enough to admit it aloud."

"True," she murmured. I fed her the other part of the strawberry. With her cherry-red kissable lips, she nibbled the last piece and swallowed. Looking down at her was another form of sensuality that turned me on. She looked so soft, relaxed, and beautiful. I could look at her all day.

"My turn. So you're thirty-five. Where do you see yourself at forty years old? What will be your reality in the next five years?"

Being that I hadn't dated in years, I hadn't heard this question in years. But from the podcasts and IG reels plastered all over the internet, I knew this was a common dating question. But I was grateful she had asked. It should me that she was interested in my future plans, perhaps to be a part of them. She was thinking of longevity. At the very least, I was hoping she was.

"At forty, I for damn sure won't be a grandfather. That's for sure." I giggled. "But a few more kids of my own isn't a bad idea. But I definitely have to be married this time around. I want to expand my electrical business in a few Caribbean islands. I'd even like to start a trade school in Guyana where I can train students and provide licensure for them to become licensed electricians. I already do a lot of charitable electrical projects all throughout the Caribbean. It's something Gianna and I do for Valentine's Day."

"Why Valentine's Day?" Eva asked, abruptly.

"Well I usually spend Valentine's Day with Gianna anyway, and usually Valentine's Day runs either on or near the week of her Winter Break, so it usually works out for us to travel during that time."

"That's cool, babe. Wow. Where did you guys go last year?"

"We went to Antigua."

"Nice."

I rubbed more oil onto my hands and continued working her shoulders, reaching down to her mid back, making sure to get into the tissue.

"Mhmm, babe. That feels good!"

I stretched my hands down her back, pushing her up into a seated position. I pushed her down, extending her back, and elongating her spine. Her bones cracked, signaling a satisfying stretch, followed by a repressive sigh.

"Oh God. I needed that."

"Yeah, you did."

I pulled her gently by the shoulders and she returned to laying upright. My hands roamed her body and ran down her leg I moved outward off the table to stretch her inner thighs. I took her body through a series of tantric stretches to relax her.

I hummed softly and methodically and she followed my beat. I could feel her limbs loosening and her body falling into a tranquil trance, as I provided her with therapeutic healing. She was one hundred percent vulnerable and at my mercy, and she trusted me by letting her guard down a bit and I appreciated that.

Within fifteen minutes of constant kneading from my magic hands, she fell asleep as expected. I listened to her light snoring as I continued working on her body. The entire time that she slept, I contemplated how I was going to pop the question. I was already doing too much, like the simp/trick that I was. Shit, I couldn't help it. I like bad bitches, that's my fucking problem. With how thick I was laying it on, already, I didn't want to pull all my tricks out of the hat too soon, but it was hard not to, especially when she was exactly my type and the chemistry between us was just growing stronger by the day.

Exhaling, I shook Eva softly to wake her up. It was primetime. I just had to do it.

After shaking her three times, she stirred, then opened her eyes and smiled. Immediately after, she yawned, sat up, and stretched her arms.

"Did I really fall asleep that fast?"

"I told you, you would. And I told you what you owe me if you did," I snickered.

"Boy, bye. Yous a freak for real."

I flashed my teeth, producing an ear-to-ear simile. "You know it. But before we get to that, I have something to ask you."

Eva's ears perked up as her brows raised. "What is it?"

Grabbing her by the hand, I licked my lips seductively "Will you be my Valentine?"

She yanked her hand away and covered her mouth. Standing up from the table, she squealed. "Oh my God. You did all of this to ask me to be your Valentine? That's so romantic babe!"

Pulling her hands from her face, and placing them around my waist, I lifted her chin to me.

"You didn't answer my question. Will you be My Valentine?"

"Of course—"

Knock. Knock.

"Daddy, are you in there?"

Alarmed, I shook my head back and forth.

"Daddy! I hear you in there. I'm coming in." Gianna's pitchy voice interrupted again.

"What the fuck? She's not supposed to be home until tomorrow." I was in full panic mode, as I looked at Eva who was naked, and heavenly-looking as can be. She looked well-rested for a long session of lovemaking. I could only imagine how much she'd be glowing after we finally did it.

"Here, wrap yourself in this robe," I said, throwing her the black silk robe from the rack under the massage table. I grabbed my cotton robe also and threw it on.

As soon as I turned around and started to move towards the

entrance, the door opened and Gianna was standing there with eyes as wide as a deer in headlights.

"DADDY! WHAT THE HELL ARE YOU DOING IN HERE?" She raged, stretching her neck, looking side to side at the erotic scene set forth. She then stood on her tippy toes to look behind me. Straining her eyes, she scrunched her face.

"Daddy, you smashing Eva the BBW Diva?"

"Gal, don't come in here questioning me. Please get out and leave me and my lady friend alone."

"Wait, Daddy that is Eva! Omg!" She shouted, and shoved past me, heading right towards Eva.

Eva's cheeks raised, looking like red balloons, as she tied the robe tighter around her torso.

Gianna wrapped her arms around Eva. "Don't be ashamed girl. No slut shaming over here, at all. I love your TikTok videos."

"What are you doing watching her TikTok videos?" I asked defensively.

"Relax, Dad. Not her sexy fitness stuff. Her body positivity and women empowerment videos. They're really good. She adds a unique perspective that needs mainstream highlighting especially as it relates to sexism and misogyny. She also promotes celibacy—" Gianna paused, and looked up at Eva, never letting go of her then said "So honestly I'm kind of shocked to find you here," she continued, directing her speech at Eva, "under these circumstances."

Gianna amazed me every day with how intelligent and forward-thinking she was. It seemed like this generation was wise and socially aware beyond their years. She constantly blew me away with her understanding of the world and how deeply profound she was, only at fifteen years old.

"For your information little girl, Eva and I aren't having sex."

"Yeah, we're not," Eva interjected, still holding onto my baby girl. I can't lie, the sight of them embraced was picture-perfect, a true Kodak moment. And so damn organic. *What the fuck was happening? And how was it happening so fast?*

"Good! Well, I'll leave you two to do whatever form of non-penetrative sexual healing ritual you were doing." Gianna articulated, finally letting go of my woman. "It was so nice to meet you Ms. Eva." Hitting me on the arm, she clicked her tongue. "You did good, Daddy. She's for keeps!"

"Bye Gianna!" Eva shouted after her as she exited the room.

"Excuse my smart-ass teenager."

Dropping her towel, her melon-sized breasts exposed and her large areolas pointing to the ground, she looked every bit of the word yummy.

"She's fine babe. It's all good."

She wrapped her arms around me, looking me passionately in the eyes.

"I bet. Since you've met your number one fan!"

"Aww, someone's a little jealous."

I pecked her on the lips. "Just a tad bit."

"Well, don't be. I'm all yours!"

"Oh really?" I asked. She was talking that talk. I needed confirmation.

"Definitely."

"So, answer two questions for me!"

"Shoot!" She said, smacking her lips together flirtatiously.

"Will you be my valentine?"

"Yes, baby, for the thousandth time!"

I cheesed dramatically, full of joy to hear her call me baby. I hadn't felt butterflies in years.

"Okay, good. Next question. Will you come with me and Gianna to Guyana for Valentine's Day? We're working on our service project out there this year, and since you two are more than acquainted now, I think it would be a good idea."

The request just kind of rolled off my tongue, although I was nervous as hell to ask. I didn't want her to think I was moving too fast, but there was no way, I wouldn't ask her to be my Valentine's properly, and with that, I knew I couldn't spend it away from her either. This trip to Guyana was already planned and the service project meant a lot to me and GiGi. I couldn't stand to disappoint either Eva or Gianna so I had to try to find a way to merge the two together.

Eva tilted her head to the side and sighed, exhaling a dramatic moan. "Are you sure about this babe? I don't want you to feel forced to ditch your plans with Gianna just to spend Valentine's Day with me. I wouldn't feel right knowing that you didn't honor a commitment made months ago to your daughter to accommodate potential plans with me."

Grabbing her hands into mine, I covered them completely with my palms. "I'm not ditching my plans with Gianna. I'm trying to include you in them. How could I ask you to be my Valentine and not spend Valentine's Day with you? What kind of bullshit is that?"

Eva nodded and pursed her lips. "You've got a point there."

"Exactly. So are you coming with us, baby?"

"Let me think about it," she said stone-faced, then busted out into a smile. "Nah, I'm kidding. Of course, I'm coming baby. I wouldn't miss it, for the world!"

Standing on her tippy toes, she grabbed me by the neck. I met her halfway and kissed her deeply. The heavy beating of my heart pumped rapidly, producing a pronounced feeling and sound that neither Eva nor I could ignore. Our kisses deepened, and our bodies melted together as we clung to each other. What we were feeling was mutual, and even more real for me, because while my boys didn't respect the fact that I was dating Eva, GiGi admired, adored, and respected not only Eva but my decision to pursue her. That right there was the green light for me.

twelve
TAKE OFF

EVA

"It's about time your ass got some dick, and the fact that it's attached to a fine ass balla who doesn't mind splurging and wining and dining you is all the better."

"How many times, do I have to tell you that we didn't have sex yet, Nika?"

With her hands on her hips, Nika rolled her neck and her eyes. "Well, shit, what you waiting for? The nigga is taking you overseas for Valentine's Day. You better give him some coochie."

It was three days until GQ, Gianna and I were set to fly out to Guyana. We'd be departing on February 12th and staying eight full days. According to GQ, he had the itinerary jam-packed with activities and events. Most of which were surprises that I'd have to wait and see, in his words. Those words were magic to my ears because I loved surprises, especially thoughtful ones. It was officially six weeks since GQ and I started seeing each other and he was wowing me every time I turned around. I hadn't been romanced like this since— well ever.

Anything that Jared ever did for me was completely erased from my memory after we broke up. He hurt me so deeply that I could never look at him the same or even think to forgive him. I pushed it so far back in my mind, refusing to settle with it, because he violated me in a way that I could have never seen coming. He robbed me of my autonomy and due to that, I wrestled with truly getting close to another man. And now that it was happening with GQ so damn fast, I couldn't stop myself.

Of all people, Nika knew that. In fact, she was the only person who knew about the bullshit Jared had put me through.

"I'm thinking about it."

"Thinking?" Nika's elevated screech pierced through my living room.

"I mean, I want to. I'm prepared to, but I'm not forcing it. So far things have been going smoothly without sex. When it happens, I want it to be organic. But of course I've got some specialty lingerie to pull out. Gotta live up to the hype of my Only Fans. You know his fanned out ass is expecting the works."

I folded my arms and twisted my lips, before licking them profusely.

"I know that's right, girl. But tell the truth. Does knowing that he's a fan bother you?" Nika asked.

I exhaled deeply. "Honestly, Nika, I thought it would bother me way more than it does. But it doesn't. It's kind of sweet that he admires me. Shit, it's been six weeks girl, and he's been doing all the right things, saying all the right things, and it just feels good, especially after meeting his daughter. As much as I want to fight my feelings, they're consistently growing."

Placing her hand on my shoulder, Nika gave me an

encouraging pat. "That's good. Allow it to grow. Don't do anything to stop the natural progression. You don't have to force anything, but you do have to be open, and that means when he's ready to slide up in you, girl you better willingly give in, and put it on that motherfucker." Tapping my wrist, she nodded. "You hear me, girl?"

I exhaled and nodded in agreement. "Yeah, girl. I got this."

"Shit, you better. With all the sexual build-up brewing between you two, I wouldn't be surprised if your ass got knocked up!" Nika cackled dramatically, while I stared back at her with a stony, unimpressed face.

Raising my hand to my temple, I tried to rub away Nika's insensitivity. I swallowed a large invisible gulp of air and just stared at Nika. Finally, she caught on, and instantly began chewing on her fingernail, before covering her mouth with her hands. "I'm so sorry E. I just got excited. I'm so sorry if anything I said triggered you, or brought about any uncomfortable feelings."

An ugly twist formed on my mouth as I crossed my arms. "Nika, you of all people know that even talking about pregnancy makes me uneasy. How could you?"

Nika exhaled deeply, tension rolling from her shoulders down to her legs. Stepping forward, she wrapped her arms around me.

"Evena, I'm sorry. Like I said, I got carried away. While I know that even the thought of being pregnant again is traumatic, especially after that bullshit Jared pulled, the truth is whether you want it to happen or not, life is forcing you to move on. God sent you someone that may be the right man to build a family with. Whether you talk about it with me, or a therapist, you have to wrap your mind around the fact that the kid conversation is going to come up, and at the rate you and Mr. GQ are going, tells me it's going to be soon."

I kissed my teeth and twiddled my thumbs. I didn't want to have the kid conversation. I just wanted to lull into the sunset with GQ and never have to address it. But I knew that wasn't logical or practical. It would come up and like Nika said I would have to come clean. It was terrifying.

"I know. I know. You're right. It's just I haven't told anyone other than you and Momma. Opening up that way to a man just doesn't seem safe. It's a part of my past that I'd rather keep buried."

Nika was a true stallion standing at six feet with a solid build. She sat down on the couch and crossed her legs allowing her size nine women's shoe to dangle.

"Love doesn't flourish with secrets or under disguise. You have to be giving of yourself and you can't do that if you're scared to open up."

I joined her on the couch and turned to face her.

"Trust me when I say opening up after you've been hurt is easier said than done."

"Nothing is easy but shit if you refuse to open up and be vulnerable, you might as well get it over with and fuck him. Girl, you're grown! If you not gon let that man love you, stop wasting your time and his!"

I was at a loss for words. Nika was never known for holding her tongue and that's what I loved about her the most because she always told me what I needed to hear especially when I didn't want to hear it.

I lowered my head and my chin sat on my double-breasted bosom. Pouting my lips, I sighed then looked up and blinked twice.

"So what do I do?" I asked.

"You finish getting yourself together and go on that damn trip. You drink, you eat, you laugh and you open up, without fear of being judged, or hurt. You smile from ear to ear, you dress your best as you normally do and if you don't remember anything I've said, remember this it's your one time to show the fuck out. You better drop it like it's hot, ride that dick like a soldier! Give him everything you've got. You've got to give him something to remember when you put it on him!"

"Your TikTok is popping girl! Three hundred thousand followers. Wow! And you're really nice with doing hair!" I praised Gianna, as we sat inside Cat Cora's, a breakfast eatery in the Jackson-Hartsfield Airport.

Gianna and I had a few minutes to talk privately since her dad was in the bathroom.

"Thank you, thank you. But my three hundred thousand followers are nothing compared to your following. You're at what, thirty million followers now on TikTok?" The gleam in Gianna's eye showed the admiration she had for me, as well as a hint of innocence. While it was evident how smart, articulate, and socially aware Gianna was, it was also refreshing to learn how open and light-hearted she was. Knowledge didn't seem to dim her light or fuel pessimism or a cynical attitude, and I was grateful for that.

Too many little black girls get hurt at a young age, whether it's from their father or mother, some ain't shit ass nigga or they hurt themselves, and turn into the most hopeless, distrustful cynics. I know because for a long time, I allowed cynicism to rule my entire personality. It took three consistent years in therapy to work through that.

"Yeah, but you'll be there in no time, with the way you're going. In fact, we should do a collab. You can do my hair in different styles, we grab some great content and get you some more customers."

Gianna's face grew uneasy as she pulled her arms tighter around her body.

"You mean followers? Because none of them are paying clients. Being that Daddy doesn't allow me to charge, I only get tips from my friends that allow me to do their hair for content. They give me between ten and thirty dollars, which is basically free. Meanwhile, this girl a grade lower than me is making bank doing sew-ins and installs. She's charging up to two hundred dollars and the girls in my school are paying. Even their mothers are getting their hair done by her." Gianna let out an aggravated sigh and shook her head. "And what's crazy is the fact that everybody knows I do hair way better than her, but being that Daddy doesn't allow me to fully operate like a business, I can't service them the times they need."

I watched Gianna roll her eyes, frustration riddled all over her face.

"I'm about to be sixteen and Daddy still treats me like a little girl." Folding her arms, she exhales deeply. "I could be a millionaire right now between doing hair, selling wigs and hair products, but Daddy is so adamant about me focusing on school and going to college."

A quick glance at my watch revealed that it had been thirty minutes since GQ was gone. While Atlanta's airport was the largest in the country and the bathroom was on the other end of the floor, it shouldn't have taken him this long to come back. Turning my head from side to side, I perused the melting pot of faces that stared into the screen of smartphones walking back and forth, lugging luggage and sipping on something whether a fancy latte from Starbucks or a cold refresher.

Returning my attention back to Gianna, I looked at her earnestly. "Do you want to go to college?"

"Honestly, I'm not sure. Part of me would like the experience of going to an HBCU and pledging to a sorority, but the bigger part of me really just wants to go to cosmetology school, build my business, work with my clients, and sell my products."

I nodded in agreement. "Ain't nothing wrong with that. From what me and your dad talked about, it definitely sounds like he will support you. I just think he wants you to explore all of your options before burning yourself out now, starting a business."

Gianna sucked her teeth. "But Eva, I'm young. Now is the time to get in the hair business, make my millions, and get out. If I start going hard now, within five years, I can retire from the chair, just sell hair, wigs, and hair products, and even do some teaching. Honestly, at that point, I can go back to college for anything, if I so choose. I just really want financial freedom."

Hearing Gianna talk was mind-blowing. This was a fifteen-year-old who already had her five-year plan mapped out. I was impressed.

"I understand, and you're right. You can definitely retire as a millionaire, and I do think you're responsible enough to start now. But you have to get licensed. Truthfully, I think that's your father's main issue. I'm sure he wants to protect you from any harm or potential lawsuits."

Gianna's head dropped into her lap like the wind from the rush of a subway train. The disappointment was displayed in her withdrawn body language. I picked her up with a finger to the chin and she straightened her back and looked back at me with hopeful eyes.

"If you really, really want to take this hair shit seriously, you should transfer to a cosmetology high school, so by the time you graduate in the next two years, you'll already be licensed. Also, you'll be able to work in the salon at the school legally, and the networking and professional opportunities that will come from legitimizing your craft now will be endless."

Zeal returned to her body, as her shoulders rolled back and a smile crept up her face. She looked more relaxed and confident as she nodded her head. Wrapping her arm around me, she squeezed me tight, as we sat next to each other in chairs. "Oh my God. That's actually a great idea. Wow, you give the best advice."

Gianna's words were heartwarming to my soul. She wasn't my child, my niece, or any kin to me, but the pure innocent love from a child was simply irreplaceable. Nothing else in the world could top that feeling. I could only imagine how it felt to get that reaffirmation from your own child. It was something I yearned the longer I was pregnant. For the short time that my baby grew inside of me, the more I became attached. Losing a baby was one thing, but having your baby stolen from your own womb without your consent or knowledge was hard to sit with.

"Look at my two girls!"

I snapped out of my thoughts quickly and raised my head.

"This one is for you, Princess Gianna," GQ said as he passed her a midsize-small bouquet of flowers and a box of Ferrera Rocher chocolates.

Gianna stood and threw herself at her dad and hugged him tightly. "Thank you, Daddy."

He leaned down and kissed her on the forehead. "You're welcome, baby."

She took her goodies and sat down. Watching him with his daughter was equally beautiful and painful. It reminded me of how many things I just never got to experience because I didn't grow up with my dad. On the other hand, it was also partly restorative to see a young girl experience the love from her dad. I smiled softly, and the next thing I knew, GQ was on his knees, in front of me.

He pulled out two velvet boxes from his back pocket and opened both. Inside each box sat a diamond tennis anklet. One had more of a classy regal look featuring small petite-sized white diamonds and the other was more urban styled, rose gold colored with chunkier diamonds. Raising my hands to my mouth, and swinging my legs back and forth like a jolly kid, I squealed wildly.

"Ouu Daddy, those are nice!" Gianna complimented.

"Oh my God, baby, thank you."

Grabbing a hold of my left foot, GQ rolled my yoga pants up and placed the diamonds around my ankle. He then placed Gianna's rose gold anklet on top of her socks that sat comfortably in her crocs.

"Ouu, an anklet!" I exclaimed, turning my foot from side to side just to examine how beautiful it looked, especially since I had just gotten a fresh pedicure and had a new pair of sandals on. It was hot as fuck in Guyana. There was no way I was flying in closed-toed shoes.

Gianna squealed alongside in her chair, rocking back and forth.

Standing up, GQ rubbed his hands together, before leaning forward and kissing me on the lips. "Damn, baby. You shining!"

Heat rose to my cheeks, and I felt my stomach squirm with feelings of warmth. That's exactly what he did to me. He was just sweet, loving, and supportive. And it was nice. Damn nice.

My eyes started to dampen and GQ laughed. "Don't tell me you're over there crying."

He took a few steps and grabbed some napkins from the canister that sat on the high table right next to him and passed them to me.

"I'm just overwhelmed with emotion. My heart just feels so full. Between you and Gianna, I just haven't felt this good in a long time."

A cute simper appeared on GQ's face, as he licked his lips seductively. He grabbed me up from the seat by my hand and into his embrace.

"Well, get used to it 'cause you fucking with BIG DAWG now!" He growled, mimicking Big Boogie, one of my favorite rappers from Memphis.

I giggled, and he kissed me and squeezed my ass firmly.

"Eww, get a room. Y'all are so tackkyyy. Uh hmm. Just no couth." Gianna complained.

We both turned around, shaking our heads, and hooted aloud.

"Mind yuh business gal and sit dung." He said, then kissed his teeth at her. "This little girl is crazy."

thirteen

FULL THROTTLE

EVA

"Thanks for understanding, baby girl," GQ said to Gianna as we walked down the aisle to board our Delta flight.

"No problem Dad. I know you and Eva need your privacy. Besides, we fly first class together all the time. I'm not tripping. You got me an entire aisle to myself, so I'm good!" Gianna sympathized. Lowering her shades to the bridge of her nose, she eyed me and GQ suspiciously. "Behave yourselves up there!"

"Likkle gal, lemme ask yuh something. Ay's yuh fadda, or yous mine? We nuh size. Mi nuh need yuh fuh warn mi fuh nuttin, yuh hear?"

"Whatever, Daddy," Gianna said, flipping him off, and quickening her step in front of us.

"Gianna is a trip. But she's so smart and sweet."

He nodded. "Yeah, she is."

"Welcome aboard." The cheeky pilot greeted us, as we stepped onto the plane.

Fancy. I guess when you're in first class, the pilots come out to greet you.

"Hi. How are you?" I asked, scanning her up and down. She was one fine woman; tall, slim, thick, and well put together, with flawless skin that made her light dewy makeup look refined and fresh.

"Great thanks for asking."

GQ passed his boarding pass to the pilot and she smiled flirtatiously. "Right this way."

She led us to the front of the plane, and as soon as she opened the door to the cabin, she turned to us and said. "Welcome to Delta One, the most luxurious cabin in all of Delta Land. Due to the courtesy of your man purchasing all of the first-class seats, he instructed us to help make this ride extra special for you two. I hope you enjoy."

As she stepped deeper inside of the cabin, I marveled at how decorative it looked. Red rose petals were lined up down the aisle. Pink, red, and white balloons were attached to the arm of each seat. In the middle of the cabin, two flatbed seats had a balloon structure draped over them, and a glass studded tray holding a bottle of Moet, two glasses, a bottle of Carolina Herrera perfume, and a tiny jewelry box that looked like only stud earrings could fit inside.

"Babe. Oh my god. How did you do this? When did you make the time to do this? WOW. I can't believe you!"

He grabbed me by the hand and squeezed it. "Chelle and I used to date a few years ago. When I told her I was boarding her flight and bought out all the seats in first class, she said she would do her best to make sure she and her crew went above and beyond to make this flight special for us."

I blinked twice, kind of taken aback by his transparency and honesty. It was a tad bit uncomfortable. *But at least he was honest, right?*

"And Chelle is the pilot?"

"Yeah. She dumped me for the man who became her husband. We're not exactly friends but we keep in touch from time to time." GQ said, as he picked up the bottle of Moet and pulled the cork out. Pouring some into a glass, he inspected every crevice of my face.

I felt the sincerity and warmth in his tone.

"From the way that she smiled at you, I could tell y'all two had something before."

He nodded in agreement. "You're right. We did have something years ago." Biting his lip, he continued. "It was steamy, it was hot. I can't lie. But that yearning for one another died when our relationship died. I moved on. She moved on." He tilted his head to the side and shrugged his shoulders. "But I guess it's natural for her to have a flashback every time she sees me. But she's the furthest thing on my mind because all I think about is you, baby girl. And dat ah real ting me ah tell yuh. For true."

"Uh hmmm." I kissed my teeth, giving him sass.

"You all good Q?" Chelle's smooth baritone alerted us both to her sudden approach.

"Yeah, everything's good. Thank you so much for doing this."

Pursing her lips into a genuine grin, she exchanged glances with us both. "No problem. There are a few business units scattered around with the gifts you requested, drinks, hor d'oeuvres, and toiletries. No one, not even staff will be allowed to enter this cabin. If you need something, text my flight attendant, Rosa. Make sure you're connected to the Wi-Fi before we take off. I sent you her number already."

"Good looks, Chell. I appreciate you."

"No problem. You guys have fun and enjoy your flight!"

I couldn't help but stare at her. She was gorgeous in a conventional, beauty pageant way. She could easily run for Miss America and win. She was about the one-hundredth woman I've met in Atlanta that looked exactly like her. I wasn't exactly intimidated or insecure, but there was clearly a stark difference between us. I was chocolate, round, sexy, and voluptuous. She was cheeky, tall, and model-esque. While we were both equally pretty and naturally beautiful, our differences made me wonder. Was I really his type or just his social media fetish?

Two hours into our flight, I was feeling nice off several glasses of Moet. I got out of my feelings, and out of my head. Learning that GQ had a prior sexual relationship with the pilot who made my first Delta One experience breathtaking was a bit of a snag, at first. But I had to respect the fact that GQ was forthcoming and honest with me. Let's be for real? GQ is fine as fuck. He's a catch. He's a good father. She has his own business, and he makes good money. Of course, he's been with many women. That was just something that came with the territory and came with being grown. Shit, I used to do webcam with strangers online. My ass is always out online, and GQ looks past all of that and still courts me and treats me like a queen. Most of all, he treats me like his lady.

I had to cut him slack. Without Chelle's help, there would have been no way GQ could have made this happen on any other Delta flight, let alone another airline. What he did was thoughtful and I refused to pick a fight about bullshit during one of the best days of my life.

"Let's go. This is the last part of the scavenger hunt. You already found your necklace and your bracelet. I can't wait 'til you see the last gift." GQ bragged.

He was so fucking sexy, from his speech; the inflection of his raspy voice, his stance, the dominance in his stride, and his lips was kissable, thick, and luscious. It was obvious that he was fine, but he was becoming more and more attractive to me, by the way he treated me. He made me feel like the most beautiful woman in the world. While I was adored by many and had tons of men infatuated, this was the first time I truly felt valued. Not just by the gifts, but the time and effort put into the experiences and his intention. To include me on a trip with his daughter last minute showed me that he was serious about me, and I couldn't let this small incident with Chelle cause me to get ultra-emotional and sabotage the love that was brooding between us.

I got up from the cabin seat with low eyes and my vision slightly impaired. Stumbling forward, I caught my balance and made my way to the right side of the cabin to find the final gift. There had been a gift on each side of the cabin; the left, middle, and right. I already found the other two on the right and left sides. There was only the middle row left. I rushed to the middle row, peeked inside the privacy seat, and didn't find anything. There was no luck with the third row, either, so I knew it had to be in the fourth row.

GQ and I exchanged steamy looks as I found a miniature velvet ring box sitting next to a black tasseled whip, a can of whipped cream, honey, and strawberries. I picked up the box, opened it, and staring back at me was a petite shiny diamond ring.

"I know you ain't proposing to me, already?" I asked sarcastically. While I appreciated all of the jewelry he got me and loved every piece, this was a bit much.

"Nah, not yet," GQ said, as he got up from the flatbed and made his way to me. "It's a promise ring."

"What are you promising me?"

"That I'll always be honest. I'll always be true. And if it's up to me, I'm hoping one-day fuh breed yuh."

I laughed so loud. "What?"

"Luk gal, mi nuh American, suh mi nuh say, 'Mi hoping fuh marry yuh one day,' me ah say, mi wan fuh breed yuh."

"Damn, shame." I joined in on the laugh. "You ain't shit!" I joked.

"Mi tell yuh, mi always gwan be honest, eh?"

Hooting with laughter, I shoved him in the shoulder. I picked up the tasseled whip and snapped him with it. "And what's this for."

"Me ah go show yuh. Let mi put on di ring pon yuh finger first," he said, grabbing the ring box, and pulling the classic diamond stud cut ring out.

Placing it on my left ring finger, he smiled. "Eh, look nice, watch wifey!" Snapping his fingers, he snickered.

I looked down at my hand and it was blinged out with a diamond tennis bracelet and a diamond ring. I peered down to my breast and caught a quick glimpse of my diamond tennis necklace. Twisting my ankle to the side, I admired my tennis anklet. I couldn't help it, but my emotions got the best of me and before I knew it, the rim of my eyes was full of water. A train of tears streamed down my right eye.

GQ grabbed me instantly, rubbing my eye with his thumb. "Baby girl, don't cry."

Him telling me not to cry made me cry harder.

Continuing to wipe my tears, GQ raised my face to his. "Baby, talk to me. What's wrong?"

"I'm happy, I'm sad. I'm just full of emotion." I cried.

"I know why you're happy but what's got you sad?"

"Exactly what's made me happy. You. Well, not you." I corrected myself. "While I'm appreciative of everything you've given me, the first man to give me this kind of jewelry should have been my father, and seeing you with Gianna constantly reminds me of that. It reminds me of what I didn't have."

GQ's eyes bulged. "Don't let what you didn't have growing up block you from enjoying everything I'm providing for you now."

I sniffled and laid my head on his chest. "You're right. Thank you, baby."

He tickled me on the sides of my tummy.

"I know I'm right. Now cheer the fuck up. We nuh doing this sad, sappy shit. We're not dwelling on the past and how your bum-ass father missed out on getting to know his jewel of a daughter. Fuck that nigga. He didn't spoil you, and it's all good because that's what I'm here to do. I'm your daddy now, and you're my baby. You hear me?"

"Yes, Daddy." I submitted flirtatiously, and for the next hour and a half, I repeated those magical words over and over again as he took turns entering my plum and my peach.

Balls deep inside my asshole, he stroked my clit from the

back, as he had his hand pressed into my head with my face plastered into the flatbed. I was overwhelmed by pleasure and from the way he warmed me up like a honey bun, my pussy was creaming and, my asshole was clenching and as equally juicy as my pussy.

Between the grunts and moans and firm taps and pinches from GQ, it was undeniable that he was in heaven as much as I was. In the past, I've done anal a few times and it was cool, but never had I craved it, shit damn near begged for it, like now with GQ. From the way he had my pussy oozing with juices and how he was working his magic thumb, massaging the walls of my peach had me yearning for him to scrap my bottomless pit.

I had already come twice. Once from him sucking tenderly on my clit, and secondly from him fucking me missionary on the flatbed. While we were cramped up in that position, the level of closeness we had took the experience to the next level. It hadn't dawned on me yet until he hit my anal g-spot that I broke my celibacy. As I screamed out, releasing a huge orgasmic holler, I shouted "FUCK CELIBACY!"

GQ chuckled as he slowed down his thrust, his dick extra lubricated with my juices, and kissed down the trail of my spine. "Facts, fuck celibacy!"

fourteen

TOUCHDOWN

GQ

The stench of salt permeated the air of Georgetown, Guyana as soon as we left Cheddi Jagan International Airport. It was a smell, reminiscent of the sea and it didn't matter how many years I stayed away, I could never forget it. Thankfully, the tangerine scent and tangy taste of Eva's pussy sat between the brim of my mouth and the bridge of my nose. Damn, that pussy, that ass, that mouth, the entire act was amazing. Eva made me feel like a man, a conqueror, and dominant.

It was better than I imagined, and she was worth every penny of the fifty thousand dollars, I've spent so far. She already had me hooked mentally, but now I was open off the pussy. It was a marvelous feeling and a wonderful experience. While I went out of my way to hit up Chelle to make the experience memorable for Eva, I really enjoyed being able to treat myself to those grand accommodations. If I hadn't connected with Eva, I would have never done anything like that, so in my eyes, it was a win-win.

"You guys look happy and relaxed," Gianna said.

"Oh baby I am," I replied, as Eva squeezed my hand tight, and giggled.

"I bet. The beds in Delta One are fire. Meanwhile, I have a crook in my neck from struggling to sleep. I'm tired." Gianna yawned.

"Well perk up. Nuh time fuh sleep. It's the family beach day. Granny, Grandpa, Tanti Ni Ni, Uncle Jam, and the kids are meeting us there at two o'clock. We've got just enough time to get to the house, shower, and eat. I'm going to get some KFC, roti, callaloo, and coconut bread."

"Yummy, Daddy. You know how much I love KFC in Guyana," Gianna said.

"What's so special about KFC in Guyana?" Eva asked.

"Ask anybody from the Caribbean and they will tell you KFC is way better in the islands than in the U.S.," I explained to Eva.

"I gotta try this because I'm not a fan of KFC at all, so if it's better here, I need to see for myself."

"Yuh gwan see gyal. Don't worry."

A few seconds later, our transport van pulled up in front of us and the doors and the trunk opened. I took my duffle bag, Eva's oversized tote, and Gianna's book bag and placed them in the trunk. Our luggage was already placed neatly in the trunk by the transport company, and I was grateful. With the way I went to town on Eva in that cabin, I was contouring my body in angles I'd never tried, I was kind of beat. A good shower, food, and beach water were exactly what I needed.

✺

"Your house is beautiful babe. And you said you have another one here, too?" I could tell from how wide Eva's eyes had bulged that she wasn't faking it. She was genuinely impressed with the latest renovations I'd made.

"Yup. I have one more vacation property in this same gated community, and another two in another community in the city of Linden. This villa was the first property I'd ever purchased. This investment property brought in so much money within the first two years, that I was able to buy my Atlanta home in cash. Prioritizing to buy an investment property first was the smartest thing I could have done."

After a hot steamy session of shower sex, Eva and I were enjoying some Guyanese street food and KFC while Gianna finished getting ready.

"That's dope. I always thought about getting into real estate but it's a lot of work, I heard, and I already have a lot on my plate." Eva added between bites of fried chicken and pholourie.

"It's really not that much work. You can pay a property manager, accountant, and business manager to handle most of the business for you. You'd just want to make sure you're checking your books, just to oversee what they report is accurate." I explained.

"Daddy! I'm ready," Gianna shouted while bolting out of her room in a sundress, flappy straw sun hat, and a beach bag hanging from her shoulder.

"Beach ready, for sure honey!" Eva praised Gianna, as she stood from the circular glass table we were sitting at.

Eva looked good as hell. She knew exactly what colors

looked best on her. She always wore colors that made her Hershey chocolate skin radiate. In an orange maxi dress that draped her body like a corset, her skin glistened like the inside of a Julie mango.

"Thank you, Eva. You look pretty too. I love your Tory Burch sandals." Gianna complimented her.

"Thanks, girl. They have a hellafied sale right now. What's your size? I'll get you a pair."

"I'm a size seven and a half. And aww, thank you so much."

"Don't thank me yet. But I got you. Babe, can we hit the mall one of these days before we leave?"

"For sure. I do need to hit the mall myself. We can definitely do that." I stood up from my seat and started to straighten up, by first gathering the food.

"Don't worry baby, I got it," Eva said, as she pulled a container of food away from me. Standing on her tippy toes, she puckered her lips and I completed the kiss. "I'm here, now. You can leave certain things to me."

Surprised, I bit my lip, looking at her with intense lust and admiration. It felt good to hear that. Just the words "I'm here" sent chills up my spine. I hadn't heard that kind of sincerity from a woman in a long time. While we hadn't made anything official, it felt like she was already mine.

"Aiight. You got it, baby," I answered and squeezed her on the ass.

"Daddy, relax. Let Eva breathe. You be doing the most," Gianna complained.

Eva and I both snickered, never taking our eyes off each other.

"I like it when your father touches me. He knows just how to make a girl feel."

Gianna's mouth dropped open and her eyes slanted to the side. "Eww. You can't be serious."

"I'm very serious. You don't mind if we share him right?"

Sucking her teeth, Gianna folded her frail arms, standing with an attitude. "Not at all. I'm finna get my own man."

My eyes darted to Gianna with an intense glare. "Likkle gal, dash way from mi. Gway! Gway! Go outside and we'll meet you out there!"

Gianna snickered and stormed off playfully. Before reaching the door, she turned around to us and said, "Just because I'm letting you rent my Daddy, doesn't mean you can have him for good." Sticking her tongue out, she teased us then turned the knob and exited the house.

"That little girl is a mess." I exhaled a deep breath and rubbed my hands together.

"She just loves her Daddy, that's all, and if I was her and had a Daddy like you, I'd love you just as much, too!"

EXPOSED

GQ

"Yous dealing wid a Guyanese mon. Mi nah care if yuh Yankee, yuh must know how fuh whine." Tanti Ni Ni shouted over the soca that was blaring from the wireless subwoofer.

Uncle Jam and his two friends snickered, as they passed a Guinness down the line until all three of them had one. Scattered in a circle were me, Eva, Tanti Ni Ni, Jam and his friends, my mom, my dad, and grandpa and grandma. Sticking my toes in the pristine white sand, I gripped Eva tighter in my arms. She was the softest thing I'd ever held on earth, and I was on her body heavy. The heat between us was electrifying as her booty sat comfortably in my crotch. Everything about her turned me on and I couldn't even hide it if I wanted to.

"Trust me, Auntie, I can whine. I'm from Queens." Eva said respectfully yet firmly standing her ground.

I grabbed her closer and kissed her on the temple.

"Gwen, yuh hea dis gal?" Tanti hopped up from her seat and popped her arm out extending her index finger. A full-on choreographed theatric experience. If there was one thing a Guyanese woman was— it was dramatic.

I snickered loudly, my laugh rolling from my belly.

"Well put yah money pon the ground gal. Leh we see eh!"

I egged Eva on by pushing her forward. "Go show 'em, babe."

Looking at me over her shoulder, she blinked softly and smiled. "Aight," she said confidently. There was a sexy glare in her eyes that intrigued me. I stepped back and watched her walk toward the center of the circle. The way her hips glided back and forth as she strutted forward had me admiring her even more.

"She wah fuh battle? Eh gal!" Tanti Ni Ni teased.

The next thing I knew Eva was rolling and bubbling up she waist in circles, up and down. She stood up, bent over, and was working her hips. She was up on her legs bouncing her ass. Everyone was cheering her on as she rocked to the beat effortlessly. Standing back in awe and admiration, I licked my lips, just imagining her naked, her gigantic melon breasts and blackberry-sized areolas ran through my mind like a lightning flash.

Tanti jumped in the circle, hyping Eva up, pumping her hands, and pointing to Eva's ass, yelling "Go gal, go gal, go gal, go gal" repeatedly.

Tanti waved me over. "Giddy, gwan get behind yuh gal now. Mi see one of Jam friend dem pon pree yuh gal," she snickered.

Barefooted, I shifted through the sand, catching a wave of the sun's reflection on the water. It was late afternoon and the sun would soon set. As soon as I got behind Eva, she bent over in the

6:30 position. Ass up, legs closed, and hands on the ground. Flashbacks of the many fetes and parties I'd grown up going to where I'd find the fluffiest girl to dagger, hit me. I placed my hand on her waist firmly and power drilled her to the hard soca beat. She took all of the pelting and even looked back at me as she took it.

Licking her lips drove me crazy. I winked and held my leg up and thrusted her from the side. The crowd of loved ones erupted into hoots and hollers. My mother and dad stood and joined in on the dance, my mom leaned over slightly shaking her rear on my dad. They were pushing seventy years old and it was a joy to see them still in love.

Family meant everything to me, and it was a wonderful feeling to know that Eva was fitting in. Most of all things were so organic and natural, yet Eva was my literal dream girl. My literal fantasy. I never thought in a million years that I would come across her ass how I had. And here we were in Guyana enjoying ourselves with my family. It felt good.

"Okay, okay gal. It seems to be mi who haf fuh put mi money dung." Tanti shouted.

Eva and I both laughed. Standing up, Eva folded her arms and said, "Yeah, gimme my money, Auntie. You were doubting the kid."

Eva's New York lingo was cute, and it made me feel like we were also growing in friendship, and comfort, which was imperative for me. When it came to committing to a woman, I needed to feel like she was my dog, too, and being that Eva was so down to earth, it was easy with her. It was enjoyable with her. It was fun with her.

After a few more songs of vibes and dancing with Eva,

Gianna and her cousins arrived back in our area. Now that they were back, it was finally time for Eva and me to have some alone time, and most of all catch the sunset.

Trying my best to sneak off without being noticed, I grabbed Eva by the wrist and pulled her in my direction.

"Hmm, sneaking off for a quick rendezvous," Tanti said loudly.

Eva and I turned around, both shaking our heads and giggling.

"Leave mi son and he bird alone," my Momma shouted, butting in.

"Thank you, Mami," I said.

"Did your mother just call me a bird?" Eva snapped, as we walked away, heading down toward the shore of the beach.

I laughed and she popped me on the hand. "What's so funny?" she asked.

"Babe, relax. My mother is really Trinidadian. Moved here as a teenager and traveled back and forth frequently. Anyway. Bird is Trini slang for girlfriend. It's equivalent to shorty. Trust mi, it's not offensive like how it's said in America."

"Better not be. I don't wanna have to curse Momma out," she joked. "Just kidding." She cleared it up real quick.

"Better be," I said, pulling her to me forcefully and smacking her ass.

Turning her head away from me, facing the ocean, Eva exhaled softly. "This view is literally breathtaking."

"We're on Bartica Island Beach right now. It's off the Essequibo River and is known for water sports, boating, and most of all its beautiful sunsets. It's no way, I wasn't bringing you here on your first trip to Guyana."

With the sun just slightly above the ocean, the sky was a hue of blue, orange, and yellow all blended into one. The smell of the ocean was just as pure, natural, and serene as the scenery.

"Thank you so much for making our first Valentine's experience together special. It's not even Valentine's Day yet and I'm already blown away. Not just by the lavishness of it all, but the authenticity and the intimacy. Meeting and gelling with your family and Gianna so organically just feels like magic, like it's meant—"

Eva's words trailed off, causing me to take my eyes off the sunset and stop and look at her. Staring into her eyes, I pulled her closer to me.

"You can say it. Like it's meant to be, right?"

"Yeah, it feels like it."

I nodded my head, and as much as I wanted to affirm her more concretely, I couldn't shake the anxiety that was rumbling along the pit of my stomach. I had to say something.

"This thing, this intimacy, this friendship or whatever you want to call it that we've been building, enjoying..." I was stumbling over my words because I didn't want to get over my head, but I also didn't want to reduce what I was feeling either. "For the last month and some change got me on a different kind of high. Got me craving you, craving all of you. But it's also got me questioning some things."

Eva's cheeks perked up as she furrowed her brow. "Questioning what, exactly?" Her entire body language had changed and her chest was now closed to me as she crossed her arms.

"Everything. The real you. Like what's the story behind you and your dad. What happened in your last relationship that you refused to talk about before? And most importantly, how do you feel about having children?"

Eva bit down hard on her lip and stepped back from me.

"See how you get whenever I try to get to know you below the surface." I pointed out.

With her arms crossed, she fumed through her mouth. "Why is it that you always want to mess up a perfect romantic night to talk about some bullshit?"

I was thrown off guard by her defiance and sass. "Getting to know you on a deeper level is not bullshit to me, and talking about your past won't mess up anything. Learning about you just makes the night more perfect to me!" I declared as I pulled her closer and ran my long fingers down the flesh of her back. Eva was irresistible to me, having switched up her hair, sporting a wavy bob cut that gave her a sultry, sexy look.

As she jittered in my arms, I could feel the goosebumps on her normally smooth skin. She took a deep breath and then looked up at me.

"I'll tell you about my dad, but that's all you're getting tonight!"

"So you're gonna make me work for it?" I flirted, attempting to lighten the mood again, although I was very serious about getting to know Eva on a deeper level. I wanted to know about her traumas, her past, and why her relationship with her dad was how it appeared to be; non-existent and or distant.

Eva winked her eye and kissed her teeth. Her shoulders rolled back and she finally looked relaxed again. "Absolutely!"

"There's one thing you need to always remember about me. I ain't scared of putting in work for what I really want."

Sheepishly lowering her eyes, her heart-shaped face looked soft and vulnerable.

Finally.

"Are you saying, I'm who you really want?" she asked.

I gasped dramatically then cleared my throat, shifting my gaze behind me, noticing that the sun had dipped lower and lower and was nearly gone. "If you aren't clear about that by now, then I must not be doing my job right then."

Placing her hand on my heart, she shook her head. "No, it's not you. Trust me. It's not. It's just this is all happening so fast, and I'm enjoying every moment. When I'm with you, I just want to forget my past. And being that you keep asking about it, it's hard to forget." She sighed deeply, before continuing. "But I know that beyond the romance if we aren't open and transparent with each other, it won't go far. And you have been more than honest with me, so it's only right I return the favor."

I took her hands in mine, so thankful that she finally felt comfortable to open up to me.

"I know who my Dad is. I'm actually very close with his side of the family. All of my cousins, even his own sister. I spent my summers in Connecticut at my aunt's house and even visit every so often now as an adult. The one thing that I appreciate my father for is his family, although it was his sister who actually made sure I was close to his side. That's neither here nor there. Anyway, my dad and I have always had a tumultuous relationship growing up, one because he was never around and was too busy running the streets and two because as I got older, his total lack of respect for me became more and more evident."

"What do you mean?" I was genuinely intrigued. "Come on let's head over there behind that rock," I suggested.

We started to walk towards the large rock that stood a few feet away on the right side of the shore.

"All kinds of shit. Just the way he talked to me, even how he answered the phone. He'd always answer the phone saying "Yo or What's Up! Whenever I did spend time with him, he'd always be on the phone, not to mention, on speakerphone so I could hear both sides of the conversation. Usually, it was him on the phone with a female." Eva rolled her eyes dramatically. I could tell she meant it with every eye stroke.

"One time, he was even having phone sex while I was sitting right next to him in the passenger seat. I felt so uncomfortable, that I cursed him out and jumped out of his car mid-traffic. I was nineteen at the time. I didn't talk to him for three years. When I finally forgave him, things were good for about a year, until one day I went by to visit him and he opened the door with an erection, and told me to make myself comfortable, that he'd be back after he finished masturbating. That right there was the last straw for me and I hadn't spoken to him since."

"Wait, what!" My lips were pursed as I cracked my knuckles. Hearing this bizarre account made me uneasy. "What kind of fucking father does and says shit like that in front of his daughter? He's supposed to respect you and protect you. What the fuck? I would never cross the line like that with Gianna. I'm so sorry you experienced that." I said, grabbing her into my arms and consoling her. I could feel the thunderous beat of her heart and her stomach contracting.

Shaking her head, a lone tear rolled down the side of her eye. "I was so tired of having to correct him and beg him to respect me, my innocence, my womanhood, and the fact that I am his daughter. It got to the point where I would constantly have to curse him out and it just became exhausting." Eva fumed and wiped the side of her eye with the back of her hand.

Continuing, Eva said, "So I sent him a text, and told him exactly how I felt. I told him he's a sad misogynistic little boy trapped in a man's body and being that he can't respect me, I refuse to subject myself to his behavior or block my blessings by constantly having to curse him out. I told him he was not invited to my wedding and that I wouldn't be at his funeral, then I blocked him. This was almost ten years ago, and he has not tried to contact me since."

I cleared my throat again and sighed deeply. What Eva had revealed to me was a lot to digest. First off, her father was a piece of shit, so I knew I had to be sympathetic to that. As someone who grew up with their dad and still has a great relationship with him, I knew that I could never truly understand how Eva was feeling or what she had gone through. More than anything, I just wanted to show her that I was a listening ear and that I cared.

"I know I blocked him, but he never ever once called me or texted me from another number. For that, I knew that he didn't care if we had a relationship or not, so I felt content knowing that I cut him off. He doesn't care about me anyway."

The hurt was visible in her downturned face, hollow eyes, and slumped shoulders. All I wanted to do was kiss the pain away from her, and a huge part of me was upset that I had even pushed her to talk about him in the first place. My baby's eyes were watery, and the fact that I caused it didn't quite sit right with me.

"Well, I can't speak for him. I can only speak for myself. I care about you Eva and I ain't going nowhere. I'm here for as long as you allow me."

Standing under the large rock statue, in the pitch dark with nothing but the sound of the ocean sweeping the shore and the beating of both Eva and my hearts, I rocked her side to side in my arms. We stayed quiet. I could tell that she was admiring the breadth of my back as she ran her hands up and down my spine while I kissed her forehead. There was no greater intimacy than what we were experiencing. Not even sex on the beach could top the rawness of naked emotion. That was more real than real could get.

sixteen

NUDE

EVA

"Yes, Daddy! Just like that. Just like that" I belted out, as GQ and I's fingers were interlocked, and his mouth was full of my sweet pussy. Bouncing between sucking on my clit, licking around the crevices of my walls, and biting the inside of my thighs every now and again, he had me in full bliss. Thank God Gianna slept over at Tanti Ni Ni's because we were loud as fuck in the house, and I was certain if they hadn't before, the neighbors definitely knew GQ's name. Well, they knew his nickname; Daddy, for sure.

Pushing his head away and squeezing my thighs together, I was overwhelmed with pleasure. GQ's tongue was as lethal as a slithering serpent. He was so skilled at eating pussy that the lapping of his tongue not only left wet trails dripping from my crotch, the consistent slurping sounded like lashes. He was whipping me with that tongue and I was enjoying every moment.

He inserted his index and middle finger inside of me, pulsing both of them in and out, his fingers were dripping wet. We had been going for the last two hours. Roleplaying, with me as the slave and him as the master. I still had my cat woman mask on, which turned him on so much, his dick stayed hard even after three orgasms. We fucked all over his room; from the bed to the floor, to the dresser, to the chair.

We were the perfect match for each other sexually. He matched my energy and I matched his. Unlike most of the men I slept with, he actually had stamina and dick control. He didn't cum in ten minutes. He allowed me to get mine, and once he saw that I was on the verge of cumming, he surrendered and we both came together in unison. Now my legs were shaking again, as he sucked on my throbbing clit over and over. I moaned, I grunted, and I even tried so much as kicking him until I just exploded.

"Ahh."

He got up from the lying position on his stomach that he sat comfortably in for the last forty minutes and wiped his mouth.

"Damn that pussy sweet!"

"And that tongue is lethal!" I shot right back at him.

Getting off the bed, he walked through the mini fridge and pulled out a bottle of water. I watched him in awe. Everything about his strong body was alluring. From his thick and toned calves to his strong, broad back and his tall neck. Not to mention those dreadlocks were becoming my favorite thing about him.

"You thirsty babe?"

I nodded and he tossed me the bottle of water. I twisted the cap off immediately and guzzled down damn near the entire bottle.

GQ's eyebrow raised as he side-eyed me. "You really were thirsty. Damn girl."

I sucked my teeth hard. This Negro was acting slow like he didn't know why. "You have been fucking the breaks off me for the last two hours, I'm exhausted."

Rubbing his chin, he snickered. "Good. Mi ah mek sure yuh feel every inch mi got babylove."

His accent sends chills through my body.

His baritone was deep, raspy yet a slow gentle whisper that was smoother than Mr. Lenny Green himself. I watched his Adam's apple protrude in and out as he gulped down the entire bottle of water. I couldn't take my eyes off of him. I was in complete lust. And to think that just a little over a month ago, I was celibate.

Part of me felt disappointed that I had broken my celibacy but the other part of me felt good about the decision I made. GQ was definitely worth giving my body to. Not only was he showing me a great time full of romance, but he was also showing me a more intimate side of him; between his and his daughter's relationship, as well as bringing me to Guyana to meet his family. While things were moving so fast, it felt natural and organic, so regardless of how or if our relationship progressed, there's no way I could regret giving myself to GQ.

Snuggling back into the bed, he spooned me from behind. His earthy aroma tantalized my senses, exciting my lady parts to where my nipples hardened, again. GQ gently brushed his fingers against my nipples as he sucked on my neck. He moved his hand down to my fupa and gripped it tightly, as he licked the inside of my ear.

I jumped in his embrace. "Babe, you're tickling me."

He snickered then sped up his tempo, moving his tongue in circular motions around my earlobe. "Good!"

After fidgeting in his arms for a minute or so, he unleashed me from his tongue, and my heartbeat slowed down. The room was so quiet, we could both hear each other's hearts. We were so close to one another, it felt like we were in each other's skin.

Breathing heavily, GQ cleared his throat. "Can I ask you a question, babe?"

The concerning tone in his voice had me a bit on edge. "Sure."

"How do you feel about children? Do you want any of your own?"

I closed and opened my eyes quickly.

Here we go again. This man just insisted on stealing the magic from the special moments we were building and it was annoying the fuck out of me.

Irritated, but trying my best to conceal it, I turned around to face him and sighed.

"I'm not trying to blow your high at all, but I think now is the perfect time to talk about kids especially since we've been having raw sex and I've been busting some big ass nuts in you." He snickered loudly, and I immediately felt a frown form on my face.

"Yes, I want children," I answered curtly and directly, hoping he'd just let it go because talking about kids was the last thing I wanted to do especially at this moment.

"How many?"

Exhaling, the fume from my nose slapped the brim of his mouth. "One, maybe. I don't know."

GQ paused for a moment, searching my entire face, then sat up in the bed. "I don't know why or what, but I feel like you're hiding something. Were you ever pregnant? Do you know if you can even have children?"

Now he was really starting to pester me. "Look, I answered

your question already. I'm open to having a kid when the time is right. Until then, I'm not worried about it. Now, can we just go to sleep? It's what, three in the morning and don't we have to be up early for the service project in a few hours?" I scoffed.

GQ's neck jerked back and he hit me with the most appalled look I had ever seen. Looking at me with bulging eyes, and nodding profusely, he stepped out of the bed. "Yeah, we can go to sleep, but I'll be in the guest room. I'm not really feeling your energy. It's very confusing. First, you're celibate, yet never really explained why. Now we're having balls-deep raw sex and you can't be real and have an important conversation with me about kids? I don't know and I don't know what kind of niggas you used to but I don't have time for the games, the secrets, or the withholding of information. I brought you out here for us to get closer, not just for sex. We could have fucked in Atlanta. But I see that you ain't ready for the level of intimacy and transparency that I'm looking for so it's no reason to pretend. I'll be in the guest room for the rest of the trip. When you ready to keep it real with a nigga, holla at me."

My mouth dropped open, as I watched him gather two of the pillows from the bed and make his way to the door.

"But what about the service project?" I asked.

"Be ready for eight a.m. Gianna and I are leaving at 8:15 sharp."

Those were the last words he said, before he walked out the door, leaving me to my roaming thoughts and an empty bed.

🔥

Just as GQ promised, he and Gianna were ready by the door at 8am. Leaning over the couch, I shuffled through my Tory Burch tote bag making sure I had everything I needed: sunscreen, wipes, and lip gloss at the very least.

"Good morning Eva," Gianna squealed as she wrapped her arms around me for a hug.

I rubbed her head and kissed her on the cheek. "Good morning baby girl."

GQ was busy spraying air fresheners around the living room.

"Good morning, baby." I greeted him, as I walked closer in his direction.

"Mawning," he said curtly, completely ignoring my puckered lips, and leaving me hanging on the morning kiss.

"Daddy, that wasn't nice." Gianna butted in.

"Mind your business, likkle gal, and go start di car," GQ demanded. "The door is open and the keys are in the console."

Folding her arms, and twisting her lip, she fumed deeply and sucked her teeth before storming out of the house.

"The last thing I want to do is have Gianna all in our business, babe. Come on. You can't still be mad about last night!"

Grabbing GQ by the arm, I pulled him closer to me. I had to use a bit of force because he truly wasn't budging.

"I'm not mad Evena. I'm just annoyed. I'm thinking you and I are getting closer, building some form of trust, but you obviously don't trust me. You're hiding something from your past and I can tell."

"Look, I'm not hiding anything. I told you the truth. I do want a kid when the time is right. What more do you want from me?"

With a stiff jawline and his arms folded, looking like an older and darker male version of Gianna, his lips were pursed and tight. "Full transparency. There were two other questions I asked, and you just glossed over them. I'm not feeling that shit. Since I've met you, I've been completely open about everything, giving all of myself to you, even the parts that hurt the most. I even told you about Gianna's mother, and you still don't feel safe to open up with me?"

I could see the frustration in his cheeks and the irritation in the bridge of his nose. It was to the point that his sinuses looked inflamed. GQ was angry and I felt bad for getting excited and turned on about him being upset.

"It's not that I don't feel safe to open up with you. I just need the space to do it on my terms. I can't be forced to just open up about deep-rooted trauma just because you've shared some dramatic shit with me. Be for real, babe. That's not fair."

GQ exhaled and rubbed my shoulders. "You're right. That's not fair. It's just I'm really feeling you, and I want to know everything about you, especially as it relates to kids and our future. Whatever it is baby, I'd rather know now to get ahead of it."

Sincerity permeated his entire being, dripping from his eyes, down to his cheeks, and mouth, and radiating upon his shoulders. *He said future. He's thinking about our future.*

"Babe, that's really sweet, but you've got to be patient with me. You can't be abrasive. I'm going to open up naturally and gradually. Ease up a bit."

"I get that you will open up naturally but this is the second or third time you've said that. This shit shouldn't be a force with us. Either you feel safe with me or you don't and real talk ma, a nigga like me ain't fighting to be your man. You gotta submit to that, and the more you resist the real shit, the more it's turning me off."

He wasn't sparing my ass at all. While he cared and was gentle, he still was persistent and demanding. Never tiring in his effort to conquer me, truly. GQ was a true Alpha. And if I was going to be with him on some real shit, as he says, I guess I'm going to have to face my shit. This was something I always knew would arise once I started dating again. The problem is I just didn't plan to start dating so soon. I was fine single, truly, but now that he's in the picture, if I want it to work, I have to open up.

"Thank you for being honest babe, and I'm sorry for being so cagey, but truthfully, I've been through some real dark, deep shit in my last relationship, specifically during the breakup that I just don't like thinking about or talking about. Especially not during a beautiful vacation in Guyana with my new man. I just want to enjoy the weather, the beaches, the food, your family, you and Gianna. I don't want to think about my past. I don't want to cry anymore. I just want to live, and I need you to live with me, not dwell with me. Do you understand?"

seventeen

CATERPILLAR

GQ

I just had to accept the fact that Eva wasn't ready to open up to me about her past. The fact that she was so cagey about it, assured me that it was worse than anything I could imagine. Yet, I couldn't think of any amount of baggage she could have that would push me away. And I just needed her to know that. But as she said, I couldn't force it. So I dropped it and we went about our morning. I was determined to let it go because I didn't come on this trip to argue with Eva. And I had to check myself because how I spoke to Eva in front of Gianna was not cool.

Without any of my doing, Gianna had a natural liking for Eva from her social media persona and she admired her. I couldn't allow my behavior with Eva to forge a wedge between me and Gianna. In less than an hour, I learned a very valuable lesson and had a true epiphany and realization of what it meant to have a daughter. Especially a growing daughter. I had to be cognizant of how I treated women in front of Gianna. Truthfully, having a teenage daughter made me question my regard for women in general. With that said, I fixed my attitude and adjusted my posture, to set the mood and tone of the day.

Because I'm a man. And that's what men do. We set the tone, and women follow suit.

We drove through the mountainous terrain of the city of Linden up to the tropics of The Pacaraima. The entire ride, we blasted music, laughed and sang. Eva let it go and everything went right back to normal. I guess it was safe to say we had our first real fight. I mean, argument. Well really disagreement. I ain't out here trying to argue with my woman. And the truth was as much as I was challenging her to grow, she was also challenging me. My usual way of applying pressure and being forceful wasn't the right tactic with Eva. Which is why she hadn't allowed me to have sex with her in her home the first time we met.

As close as we got, she still held back, and I had to respect that because the way shit happened between us was crazy. And I knew for a fact that another woman would have easily let me smash that night, especially with how aggressive I was. Eva made me slow down. She's always making me slow down. It's like she's a tough yet tender slab of meat that has to be slow-cooked for hours and hours.

Parking the Jeep Wrangler in the grass, alongside a line of cars, I rolled the windows up and pressed the button to put the top on.

"We're here, Ladies. Wake up." I announced, shaking Eva's thigh gently.

Her eyes opened immediately and she smiled softly. I turned around and shook Gianna's leg. "Baby, girl wake up."

Gianna rose from her slumber and stretched her arms.

"Babe, where are we?" Eva asked as she opened the door and stepped out of the car.

"Paradise. We're at the Pacaraima, also known as the Pakaraima Mountains. I used to come here all the time as a teenager, and rip and run wild."

Eva turned around in a full circle. Her hands covered her mouth, as she admired the view. "This is breathtaking. Wow, babe."

"Babygirl bring everything you brought with you. We won't be back for a few hours." I told Gianna, halfway telling the truth but mainly lying. We weren't going to be back for a few days with the surprise I had up my sleeve, which was the main reason Eva and I needed to make up, so we could truly enjoy Valentine's Day together.

I stepped out of the car, admiring the open plain view of green asphalt-covered mountains that surrounded us, drowning our eyesight of anything beyond the jungle we were in. The sound of faraway waterfalls was persistent in the air, along with clouds that looked close enough to reach. It was a truly breathtaking sight and I was determined to have a wonderful time with the two leading ladies in my life. I walked around to Eva's side of the car and grabbed her from behind.

"Where are we again? What mountains?"

Pressing my lips into the side of her face, I planted a deep kiss on her cheek. "We're at the Pakaraima Mountains, which spans from southwestern Guyana into Brazil and parts of Venezuela. We're going to be helping an organization pave some of the roads that connect to some major highways in Guyana."

I told Eva that I brought her on this trip to get closer to her which is definitely true. But I specifically brought her on this service project with Gianna to see what she was made of. I knew she didn't want me or need me for my money, she had enough of that. I knew she was smart and of some substance, but what I truly needed to know was the position of her heart. Was she the kind of woman that could impact the world with me? Did she care about others outside of herself and was she willing to give of herself?

All of those things mattered to me when it came to choosing a woman. After Gina left me and Gianna, I spent a lot of time alone preparing for now; where I found a woman I truly wanted to invest in. I needed to know who Eva was at the core. I needed to know her character, and this was the perfect opportunity to learn more about her.

"Interesting. Wow," she responded.

I could tell that she was intimidated but she didn't express disinterest. I think she was just curious about how we would be contributing and helping. And truly so was I. This was my first time doing this kind of service in Guyana. We normally worked in the ghetto cleaning up or near the landfills, helping with electrical wiring, and making sure the electricity towers were running smoothly. I normally did the electrical work by myself and only brought Gianna along to clean up, but when I saw this opportunity on the website, I thought it would be great for Gianna, and Eva.

"Bring your bags with you, and come on babe."

The drive through the forest, to the other side of the mountains was as breathtaking as it was to watch Eva and Gianna enjoy every moment of it. The first part of the service project included an hour-long tour of the perimeter of the mountains where we saw beautiful rock lakes that bordered residential areas where homes were scattered about. Whenever the sound of a herd of goats was near, that seemed to signal that we were embarking on a residential area. Then five minutes later, we'd be galloping up a rocky hill of dirt, while chasing the endless greenery surrounding us. It seemed like the higher we drove up the mountain, the closer the sun felt.

Eva squeezed my hand, as the transport van jerked to the side while narrowing a sharp corner of the terrain.

"We're two minutes away from our location, guys. Don't worry we will be out of this stuffy van in the next two minutes." The project organizer who sat in the passenger seat of the twelve-seater van warned us.

The car parked shortly after, and we got out of the van which was parked on the grass. Me, Gianna, Eva, and the rest of the volunteers stood alongside each other, as we all took in our surroundings. Another breathtaking sight.

"First off, I'd like to start by thanking each and every one of you for taking the time during your vacation to help serve the citizens and residents of Guyana." The organizer was a short Peruvian man with oily skin and long oily jet jet-black hair. According to his speech-delivered bio, he has spent all of his adult life, a total of thirty-two years working in grassroots eco-development.

"Without the dedication of hungry charitable servers like yourself, projects like this would be impossible to complete. As you know the service project is only three hours long and you will help with mainly parting the red clay for the road pavement to be done by the contractors. It is very easy, so please do not be intimidated. No one here is expected to be a professional. Now, to the left of us are gloves, sun-shielding glasses, and shovels. Please grab one of each, and put the sunglasses and shades on."

After the entire group was suited up, we followed the organizer to the working area and watched him show us what needed to be done. He was right. It was pretty easy. Eva came prepared with a bonnet and wrapped her hair up. She even brought an extra one for Gianna which made me smile. That was the kind of ghetto down-to-earth shit I loved about black women. Who the hell wanted all kinds of bugs and debris in their hair? Red clay wasn't too bad but all the other shit was of no good use to their hair.

The organizer left us to ourselves and we got to work. Gianna, I and Eva were in a group by ourselves while two other groups of four were scattered about the landfill near different ends of massive piles of red clay. I watched Eva plant her shovel into the red clay pick up a heap of it and slap it down on the empty paved road. She then proceeded to smooth it out with her shovel, making sure that it was evenly distributed.

"Daddy, look!" Gianna shouted.

I shifted my gaze to Gianna who was following the same routine as Eva, smoothing her red clay onto the pavement as neatly as possible.

"Go GiGi. That's my GiGi," I sang to the tune of Lil Wayne's infamous *Go DJ* song.

Her electrifying smile warmed my heart as she continued working. Returning my attention back to Eva, I admired her strength and commitment. At the speed and intensity that she was moving it was easy to see that she was into it, and I appreciated that. I placed my shovel down, and stepped behind Eva, wrapping my arms around her, and steadying my hands on top of hers, both of us gripping the shovel.

I kissed her cheek and trailed my lips up to her ear. "Thank you for being here and doing this with me babes."

The sides of her face filled out, pressing against mine. I knew that smile was bright and big. I could feel it.

Eva turned and faced me. "Thank you for bringing me baby. I've never done anything like this in my life. It feels really good to be contributing to society in such a profound way. I have a newfound respect for how people live outside of the U.S. This is a beautiful experience."

"That makes me feel good to hear that, and honestly it's what I was hoping to hear. I love my country so much and I just feel compelled to give back in the ways that I can- like acquiring real estate, and land and helping the country in ways that do not benefit me at all but benefit the greater good of Guyana."

Eva shook her head and chuckled. "Who are you? Like is this even real? I've never met anyone like you."

"And you never will. Just stick with me and you'll always have the original. The blueprint."

We kissed, with the sun dawning down on us. I rubbed my hands from the cuff of her ass up and through her bonnet. We were so lost in the moment. The only thing bringing us back to reality was Gianna's pestering shouting.

"Guys this is getting embarrassing. All this PDA, puh-lease have some respect for the minor over here." Gianna stammered.

"Oh please. You like to pull that minor shit when it's to your benefit. Gal be happy to see love. Know that you shouldn't expect anything else than what you see me doing for mine. You too are mine, so when it's your time to choose, make sure his heart is big, his money is long and his love for you is enormous and actionable. You hear mi, gal?"

Gianna nodded her head submissively. "Yes, Daddy."

After handling Gianna, I faced Eva and she was staring at me with beaming eyes and admiration.

"I just love how you are with GiGi. It's so adorable. I commend you for being a great father."

Eva sure was pulling on my heartstrings. It was nice to hear that although Gianna didn't have a present mom, I was doing a damn good job as a father. Being a father is the most important job that I have and I don't take it lightly.

"Thank you, baby, for saying that. You're the first woman I've brought around my daughter, and I don't regret it. I'm actually happy her nosey self stumbled in on us."

Eva popped me on the arm. "Shh, hush. Don't bring that up."

"Eva, please. Gianna's not stupid. She knows what was going on."

My baby girl nodded her head eagerly. "Sure did. You were breaking your celibacy with my Daddy," Gianna blurted out.

We all started laughing, Eva included.

Gianna's shoulders rose as a whimsical grin painted her face. "What? What did I say?" She giggled repeatedly.

"Nothing, nothing, just get back to work, and stay out of grown folks' business."

"Whatever, Daddy. You ain't got no business."

"Likkle gal, dash way from me." I threatened her playfully with an exaggerated backhand motion. With her shovel in hand, she scurried down a few feet scooped up a pile of red clay, and got back to work.

Me and Eva laughed and continued working.

After three hours, we all had finished what we could, and the project organizer was reeling us in. I was excited to reveal the surprise to Eva.

"Wow, look at that. The time is gone already. And look at what you've done. Give yourselves a hand." The project organizer clapped loudly and all twelve of us joined in on the clap.

"We will email each and every one of you your certificate of service and a link to all of the photos our photographers took. Thank you again for your service. Now, the part that everyone has anticipated, and for some of you it may be a surprise. As an incentive for your service, everyone here is awarded a one-way trip to Brazil on light aircrafts provided by The Pakaraima Mountains Association. The flight is only two hours which is why we told you to pack very light."

"What?" Eva squealed, followed by excitement from some of the other travelers who weren't aware of the incentive either. "I'm going to Brazil? We're going to Brazil?"

"Yeah, baby we're going to Brazil."

"Daddy, I'm so excited. I can't wait to go to Iguazu Falls!" Gianna rambled, for the thirtieth time. She knew we were going to Brazil months ago and talked my ear off about Iguazu Falls nonstop. I asked her to keep it a secret once she knew Eva was coming so I could surprise her. My baby girl was really a great sport, for allowing me to share our tradition with Eva. And Eva was a great sport to be willing to share me with Gianna on our first Valentine's Day. But I was determined to make it really magical and special for both of my girls but most especially, my leading lady Eva.

CACOON

EVA

"**G**irl you are glowing!" Nika shouted through the FaceTime video. "Brazil sure looks good on you, chile."

I cackled, studying myself in the camera. She was right. My Hershey skin was radiating in the apple green dress draping my body. The contrast between my skin, the garment, and the ocean-side view was electrifying.

"My man took me shopping in Rio De Janeiro. Clock it bitch, ahh kay."

Nika twisted her lip and sucked her teeth. "You see what giving up a little cootie cat ah get yuh. Trips to Brazil, shopping sprees. Yeah, bitch!"

"There you go. Everything ain't about sex, Nika." I snapped. "He had this planned before we even had sex. In fact, this trip was planned with his daughter and really he included me. And that's because he fucks with me like that." I corrected her. Yeah, I was a bit defensive because I knew what me and GQ have is more than sex. "We have a friendship and a bond. Me and his daughter have a bond. He put it on me in such a way that superseded anything sex could do. He takes his time with me, he listens to me."

"Okay, okay you got it. I'm not tryna argue with you girl. I'm just happy for you is all. You're too young and too fine not to be giving up that good pussy to a real nigga like him. In other words, keep doing exactly what you doing baby!"

I rolled my eyes playfully and licked my lips. "Oh I will."

"As you should! Where's Gideon at anyway?"

It cringed to hear her call my man by his government name but I also didn't know how I'd feel about her calling him his nickname GQ because she doesn't know him on that level. I swallowed hard, and quickly closed and opened my eyes. I was really feeling this nigga getting all territorial and shit, even with my own friend. *Damn, E you gotta chill.*

Snapping out of my possessive thoughts, I replied, "He went to wash his hands. He got some sticky sauce from these bomb-ass appetizers on him."

"Ahh okay. Well, baby girl happy Valentine's Day again. Let me wrap up here at work so I can meet Tyson I'll take pics and send you, although I know nothing here can compare with Brazil but my baby tries, he sure does," Nika giggled.

"Happy Valentine's Day, girl. You and Tyson enjoy. Love you." I said ending the call.

It didn't matter how much Nika and I went back and forth aggressively that was my girl. My dawg for real, and I knew she was happy for me.

A minute later, GQ came strolling out from the back of the

ocean-side restaurant where the bathroom was. It was almost six p.m. and the sunset looked marvelous but not as good as my man. GQ was wearing a cream linen suit that was tailored so perfectly to his lean, built body. Paired with a crisp white tee, one of those five hundred dollar white tees, my baby was looking like money. No wonder he made a dash to the bathroom as soon as he got dirty. Before sitting down he leaned over me and planted a warm kiss on my lips.

"You always taste so fucking good," he moaned as he took his seat.

I blushed, heat rising to my cheeks and a chill rolling down my spine to my nipples.

"You're just a natural at this shit, ain't you?"

"A natural at what? Treating my lady right?"

With a tilt to the side and a scratch to the chin, I thought about his question. I guess it really was just that simple. GQ had come into my life at such an unexpected time when I wasn't looking for anyone or anything, and I wasn't able to resist him. He didn't allow me to say no, which I was grateful for because had I pushed him away I would have missed out.

"Yeah, you are."

"And it won't ever change. I'm not saying I'm perfect or that we won't have disagreements in the future, but that will never dictate how I treat you. You're my lady, and there's nothing I won't do to keep you smiling, happy and comfortable."

My belly was full of butterflies that had me on cloud nine. I was overwhelmed with romance. When would it stop? Every time I turned around, it was another surprise. Another thoughtful, breathtaking experience. More intimacy, more kisses, more hugs, more… love. I was enjoying every moment but the looming anxiety in my mind was waiting for something bad to happen or for GQ to disappoint me in some way. Because of course, this was too good to be true.

As I stared off behind GQ fixating my gaze on the patrons at the bar, my eyes bulged at the site in front of me. The entire time I was on the phone with Nika, I was watching this strange-looking couple at the bar. What was most strange about them was their interaction. The girl was young, somewhere in her early twenties, which wasn't hard to tell. Between her overtly revealing clothing, and her entire back out paired with the shortest coochie cutters I've ever seen, it was evident that she was a college student. From the way she wore her hair, a frontal lace wig with the swirly baby hairs, I could tell she was from the US. Her date, an older white male looked very suspicious. He was wearing a baseball cap, a long-sleeved off-white shirt, and cargos.

I had kept my eye on them while on the phone because I could have sworn he looked just like one of those abductors from the movie Taken. And what I just saw got a rise out of me so quick. My palms started sweating, my hands were shaking and I couldn't stop myself. I got up from the table slowly, and GQ's eyes followed me.

"Where you going, baby?" He asked.

I ignored him and made my way over to the bar where the strange white man was sitting. The young black girl must have gone to the bathroom because she was nowhere to be found. I can't believe in a busy restaurant like this, he would even try that bullshit. I exhaled deeply, my eyes full of water. My chest was tight as my mind went to a traumatic experience I tried so hard to bury. Balling my fists up, I punched the man three times in his back and slammed his head into the island in front of him.

Nose bloody, he jumped up in a rage. "What the fuck!" He

yelled in a crunchy Italian accent. "You stupid bitch." He
flinched at me and before I knew it, GQ was standing in front of
me. He swung two smooth punches and the man fell to the floor.
A commotion broke out in the entire restaurant as everyone
watched us with gawking stares.

A security guard and a few members of the staff shuffled
toward us, swatting their arms.

"Everyone, OUT NOW, before we call the police." A guy
who looked like the manager because his English was the best
I'd heard all day and he was dressed pretty Americanized, said.

Pulling me to the side forcefully by the arm, GQ clearly
looked confused. "Baby, what the fuck? What's going on? Why
did you attack that man?"

Everything in me wanted to scream and cry until the tears
just couldn't flow anymore. I wasn't sad. I was frustrated. I was
angry. I was mad.

With tears streaming down my face, I blew out hot air
repeatedly. I was damn near hyperventilating.

"That man!" I spat out, trying to regain my breath.

"Babe, talk to me, what's going on?" He asked, as he patted
my back and rubbed my shoulders, helping me to relax.

"That man must be some kind of trafficker because I saw him
putting something in that girl's drink."

"What girl?" GQ asked with a dumbfounded look on his
face.

I turned around and pointed towards the bar where the staff
and manager were cleaning up. The young girl had returned to
the bar and was just as surprised and confused as GQ. Luckily
the staff had cleaned up the area, moving all the glasses and
plates they were using, including the drink that had been
tampered with. GQ and I were standing on a small bridge that

connected the resort to the restaurant and beach, and we were able to see everything.

GQ sighed and chuckled lightly. "Let me find out you're a vigilante too, girl. You had me scared as fuck. The way you charged over there, without saying anything, had me thinking you were bipolar or some shit. Damn, that's crazy. Thank God you did see it or that girl would have woke up the next morning out of it. But babe, doing shit like that is risky and dangerous. What if I wasn't here to protect you? What then? You gotta be careful and use discernment before making a crazy move like that."

"What I did wasn't crazy. What that pedophile was trying to do was!" I switched my hips and placed my hands on them. He had no idea how watching some shit like that was traumatizing for me, and here he was calling me crazy.

Reaching for my hand, he said: "You know what I mean, baby."

I slapped his hand as I was infuriated. Today was Valentine's Day and it was supposed to be special, but things were not going according to plan. Of all days, today had to be the shit show.

A well-put-together couple walked past us, hand in hand. At first glance, the woman was gorgeous and model-like, and the man was equally as attractive. GQ's eyes followed them both until an anxious look covered his entire face. Cracking his knuckles and biting his bottom lip, he fumed deeply.

"Eva, go back to the suite" he asserted.

I sucked my teeth and rolled my neck. "Huh?" I was thoroughly confused.

"Go to the suite with Gianna. There's something I need to handle." He repeated himself, and with a determined swift bop,

GQ trudged off, leaving me to myself with a scattered mind and a discombobulated heart. *What the fuck was going on?*

FACE-OFF

GQ

I had five seconds to calm down before I lost my cool or before they turned around and discovered me. I was too late, and he turned around and eyed me with a puzzled look. I was on their heels, close enough to know that I wasn't bugging. That was her. The man she was with turned back around and grabbed her closely by the hand. I didn't give a fuck, if he was her husband or not, I needed a word.

"Gina!"

They both stopped in their tracks and turned around.

"Babe, you know this guy?" From a quick look at him, I knew he was her husband. He looked just like the Cuban nigga I'd seen in pictures that the private investigator showed me a few years back. Bald, with a thin trimmed goatee and a cigar in his hand. He definitely looked like an older version of PitBull.

"Yeah. I'm just the nigga taking care of her fifteen -year-old daughter that she abandoned to be with you and play house with her other kids."

Gina's rosy cheeks burst through her makeup, as her jaw started to jitter. "Baby, give me and him a minute to talk alone."

He eyed me up and down and took a long pull from his cigar. "Baby, you sure?"

"Yeah."

"Okay, I'll be right by the bar where I can have a good look at you."

"Okay, baby."

The two lovebirds exchanged kisses as I stood there twiddling my thumbs. Pitbull's grandfather sucked his teeth as he looked at me with a nasty scowl. I didn't bother to get riled up with his ass when this shit with Gina had nothing to do with him, but everything to do with the little girl we shared together.

"So, you're enjoying another Valentine's Day, without a care in the world about your daughter?"

The disgust that permeated my heart blocked my eyesight, to the point where I couldn't even acknowledge Gina's undeniable beauty and how well she was put together.

"Gideon, she's sixteen, like you said. How long do you think guilt trips are going to work? If I didn't care when she was six, what makes you think I give a fuck now that she's sixteen?"

Those words hit me like a rod but, it was her body language that said it all. She could give not a fuck about her own flesh and blood that came out of her.

"Maybe the fact that you didn't have a mother growing up yourself, and would want to stop the cycle from continuing but I guess that doesn't mean shit to you either."

Dressed in a white swing dress that accentuated her sculpted calves, she looked flawless, as I'd always remembered her. She

147

was aging gracefully considering that she was ten years older than me and I hadn't seen her since Gianna was eight years old. But the ugliness from her heart ruined it all.

"Look Gideon, I told you a long time ago, when you first tracked me down, that I wasn't interested in being a mother. So what is this all about?"

"So you weren't interested in being a mother to Gianna, but you can be a mother to them kids with that Spanish motherfucker? You really ain't shit."

Pursing her lips and gripping her clutch so tight, the bones in her fingers appeared engorged.

"That Spanish motherfucker is my husband. That Spanish motherfucker also has a net worth of nine hundred and thirty-five million dollars and I didn't have to sign a prenup."

"Right, how could I forget how much of a gold digger you are, especially after meeting you in a strip club?"

Gina shrugged dramatically and shifted her weight from side to side. "I have no fucking idea. All I know is that things turned out for the best. I got away from your frugal ass and bossed up with a man who not only made me a multi-millionaire but an honest woman. See, the kids I have at home were made in love, in wedlock, not survival or a product of sin like Gianna. And most importantly, their father is a very, very wealthy man, unlike you. I mean I know you're doing decent with that electrical work you've been doing for a while. Yeah, I've looked into you too, but you couldn't wire enough homes or sign enough corporate contracts to even get close to what my man, excuse me, husband brings in a month. Now if that didn't answer your—"

Control was slowly slipping away from me, and I lost it. I slapped her across the face hard and fast, and my hands instantly went to her neck, wringing her tighter and tighter. I felt like I was in a trance. I couldn't see or think straight. All I knew was my eyes were getting watery and my vision was becoming cloudy. Out of nowhere, I stumbled to the side and tripped over my foot.

Pitbull punched me on both sides of my face and almost knocked me out, but I quickly restored my balance and squared up. Gina's husband had taken off his suit jacket and was circling around me. With all my might, I charged at him, knocking him down. I pounced on him like a cheetah with the speed of thunder and went to work on his ass. I unleashed blow after blow until I was dragged off of him by three large men.

"Bro, get the fuck out of here now, before the policia comes," one of the Brazilian guys warned me as I rubbed the sides of my face. Gina was holding Pitbull by the arm, inspecting his wounds with the utmost care, meanwhile, her daughter needed a mother and she could give two fucks. I couldn't believe I let myself go like that but she hit several nerves, the biggest referring to Gianna. I could accept all the shit she said about me, but referring to my baby girl as a product of sin was a slap in the fucking face.

My heart was breaking for my baby girl. That her own mother could reject her so coldly. That her own mother could turn her back on her. How was I supposed to tell my baby girl that I ran into her mother in Brazil with her new husband and she didn't ask to see her, and that she insisted on never seeing her? I couldn't do that.

I didn't even have the strength to face Gianna. I didn't have the courage. At this very moment, all I wanted was Eva's warm embrace, comforting me. Her listening ears hearing me, and a kiss from her that could heal it all; the hurt, the despair, the confusion. Advice that would make a difference. I just knew something profound would come from her lips that are rich in wisdom but taste like honey.

I regained my footing, by cracking my neck and eyeing my surroundings. The sun had set and the Oceanside restaurant was dimly lit. Bright lights dawned over the ocean that was scattered about in homes off the hills and mountains afar. Taking one last look at Gina, whose neck was red and bruised, and the side of her face with a handprint, I knew it was time to get out of there.

And that I did, expeditiously.

NAKED

EVA

I was rocking back and forth, displeased with myself for how much lying I did to Gianna. I spent twenty minutes mulling the story over and over in my head to make sure it made sense and wouldn't cause her to become alarmed. I deserve an Oscar award because she was so chill and sucked up every fib I told, completely enthralled with my company, that after three hours, she fell asleep without even asking about her dad.

In the time that we spent together, it was obvious that she was yearning for a mother figure or at the very least an auntie or older sister. The way her eyes beamed up as she shoved her phone in my face, showing me the latest viral hairstyle on TikTok seeking my validation, told me everything I needed to know. She yearned for a mother as much as I yearned for a dad. And it seemed like my relationship with her father was healing the inner child in both of us.

Nonetheless, after she went to sleep, I was completely alone with my thoughts. Flashbacks of me waking up in a pool of blood on my mattress and leaning over the tub as blood clots gushed out of me ran through my mind. The pain was unbearable physically and mentally, especially because when it was happening, I had no idea what was going on. Had I known I was having an abortion I wouldn't have been so alarmed. I would have been prepared for the pain but I was totally unaware. And seeing that man try to drug that girl triggered something in me that I thought I dealt with a long time ago. The year of therapy I attended just didn't help I guess.

And now I had to explain it all to GQ, on Valentine's Day. The day we should be in bliss, we were both more confused than ever. I knew my behavior at the restaurant threw him for a loop, and the way he ditched me while I was feeling most vulnerable had me puzzled. I didn't know what to think. While I thought we were getting closer, apparently we were being pulled apart. And the fact that it's been hours since he's returned has me on edge.

How did everything go from perfect to a shit show in a matter of minutes? I was tired of sitting, so I stood up and started to pace the perimeter of the suite's living area. Lavish was an understatement. From the marble flooring to the grand antique furniture, we were staying in an Old Latin-decorated resort. Everything screamed Spanish colonial home, from the brass glass drop chandelier to the textured walls, and heavy furniture. As I paced back and forth, my feet rubbed against the red floral area rug. The twisting of the knob of the front door startled and excited me at the same time.

He was finally back!

I softened my face and relaxed my shoulders because the last thing I wanted to do was go ballistic. However, the old me would have felt like it was completely warranted especially since he had disappeared for the last three hours, leaving me all alone at my most vulnerable moment. But I knew that I had to approach this differently.

He stepped inside the house, and his entire body dragged. His rigged posture and slumped shoulders made him look shorter. His eyes were flushed, his gaze flat. I had never seen him like this, and all I wanted to do was soothe whatever pain he had been feeling. It was obvious something happened and I needed to know.

I stepped closer to him and wrapped my arms around him, and the weight of the entire world fell on me. His heavy head rested on my shoulders, as I rubbed his head. His heavy breathing, accompanied by light crying startled me.

"Baby, what's going on? What happened?"

After several moments of silence, his arms gripped around my waist tighter and tighter, and he finally let me go. His eyes were red from the crying and I could tell he was ashamed. He grabbed my hand and motioned me over to the sofa. Sitting down with my hand in his he sighed.

"I saw Gina. Gianna's mom."

I gasped. "She was the woman with that man that we saw?" I asked as images of a very attractive couple jogged my memory.

He nodded. "Yes, that was her."

"Okay, baby. Tell me what happened."

He inhaled several times before exhaling a long sigh.

"I don't know why I even approached her. I don't know why I expected her to suddenly care about her daughter, but seeing her made me want to try. I was thinking maybe if she saw Gianna, she'd fall in love with her just as I did. I thought maybe seeing her daughter would change her heart. But I was wrong."

Never taking my eyes off GQ, I stood from the sofa and scurried to the mini glass bar that stood behind us. I poured him a large glass of red wine and passed it to him. He took it gladly and swallowed several sips before placing the glass down on the table.

"Thank you. I needed that."

"No problem, baby. Continue telling me what happened."

He narrowed his eyes and pursed his lips while tilting his head to the side. "Just like she told me years ago, she never wanted to be a mother. But she made it super clear that she doesn't want to be Gianna's mother. She said some bullshit about Gianna being a product of sin because we weren't married and that she's a mother to her kids now because her husband is a billionaire. Hearing that she disowned my baby girl because of me, caused me to lose it. I slapped her and I nearly choked her out and then fought her husband."

Hearing his grief broke my heart. While his reveal of violence was startling, I was only concerned with his heart.

Searching my face, he grabbed me by the hand. "Look Eva, I know I shouldn't have put my hands on Gina and I need you to know that I have never laid hands on a woman. I don't know what took over me," he confessed. Tears were now gushing from his eyes.

I was stunned and didn't know how to feel, so I did what came naturally to me. I scooched closer to him and wiped the tears from his face. I gently kissed up and down his cheek until I felt his quickened heartbeat settle down.

"I could only imagine how hearing that made you feel, not just for you, but mainly for Gianna. I'm sorry she said those things. Most importantly, I'm sorry that she's missing out on having a relationship with her beautiful, articulate, intelligent daughter."

"Yeah, but she's not sorry. She doesn't see the issue with Gianna growing up without a mother's love, although you would think she'd sympathize since she also grew up without a mom, but instead of forcing her to do better, in turn, it made her more cold." Nostrils flaring, GQ twisted his lip and lowered his gaze. "And I'm the one that has to pick up the pieces of Gianna's heart time and time again when the mother conversation comes up. I'm the one that has to keep the lie going that her mother is still strung out on drugs, and nowhere to be found. I can't tell a sixteen-year-old that her mother is a gold-digger and abandoned her to go be a mother to three other kids. I can't tell her that I ran into her mom in Brazil with her husband and she didn't want to meet her. I can't fix my face to tell the little girl that takes up the space of most of my heart that she's not even good enough for her own mother's love. I just can't." He expressed then broke down into an emotional sob.

I stood on my knees on the couch and hovered over him, covering him with all of the tender loving care inside my entire being. I just wanted to take all the pain away, he was feeling, and I knew nothing I could say would do that. Just being there, holding him was enough, and I knew that because that's exactly what I needed. No advice, not trying to help me dissect anything. I just needed him just like he needed me.

GQ pulled away from me and wiped his eyes. I stood up and grabbed a box of tissues from the end table and passed him a tissue. He wiped his face.

"Pass me another one."

I did and he blew his nose profusely, sounding like a haggard horn. "Sorry, babe," he chuckled.

"It's all good," I laughed back. "That's what the tissue's made for."

"Eva, I don't know how long we're going to be in each other's lives, but I just want you to know how much I appreciate you being here, now. At this moment. With me."

A warm smile stretched to both sides of my mouth.

"But I'm going to ask you something." The shakiness in his hands had me on alert.

"Sure, babe. Anything."

"Well, two things. First, I need your word that you will never and I mean never tell Gianna about tonight or anything about her trifling ass mother."

He was holding onto my hand so tight I knew he was as serious as cancer.

I nodded in agreement. "You have my word."

"Good. Now the next thing, what the hell happened back there with that guy you attacked? I know you said you saw him put something in a girl's drink, but I don't know, the more I think of it, the more I know a lot is missing from what you did tell me."

It was now or never. I couldn't just shrug it off. I couldn't just avoid it. I couldn't hide. He laid everything out on the table and it was my turn.

"You're right. There's a lot I haven't told you and it goes back to our earlier conversation about kids."

GQ was listening eagerly as he interlocked his hands with mine. "I'm here, baby."

"I was pregnant before. Four years ago. And I was ecstatic about having the baby. My boyfriend Jared of two years seemed happy too. Two weeks after telling him, he started to become distant. He moved out, without telling me. One day, I just came home and his stuff was gone. For weeks I hadn't heard from him. At eleven weeks pregnant, I got a call from him, telling me he was sorry for going ghost and that he wanted to be with me and he wanted to be a father. He asked me to meet him for lunch, the next day. The entire time I drove to the restaurant, I felt something in my gut tell me that he was lying and that he didn't want to be with me. At the moment, I just made it up in my mind that I was going to be a single mother and I was okay with that because I was already attached to my baby. If I had known that what he was going to do was worse than being an absent father, I would have never gone to meet him."

I picked up GQ's glass of wine and drank the rest. I didn't have the energy to pour myself my own glass so this would have to do. He watched me consume each and every drop of the remaining remnants of his drink with soft, sympathetic eyes before taking the glass from me. Water was starting to fill my eyes, so I wiped away the tears with the back of my hand.

"When I got to the restaurant, I could just tell that something was up with him, but I couldn't put my finger on it. So I just sat and listened to his bullshit excuses, and ate lunch. When I first got there, there was a glass of water on the table, and I remember thinking it had a weird acidic taste to it. I brushed it off, thinking it was my hormones or extra acid in the water since it was from the tap. Anyway, the next morning, I woke up in excruciating pain with blood all over the mattress, and blood clots coming out of me. I felt like I was going to die. Anyway, when I got to the hospital, I was told that I was having a miscarriage. However, they kept me in the hospital for three days, and after running tests, I was told that I was actually having a miscarriage and had been drugged with both Mifepristone and Misoprostol, the names of the abortion pills."

It felt like a boulder was lifted from my shoulder. I had never revealed this to anyone but Nika and my momma. It felt good to finally release it.

"Baby, I am so sorry that happened to you and I completely understand why you didn't want to talk about kids. That shit that nigga did was foul. I never heard no shit like that. His ass should be locked up," GQ said as he grabbed my legs and placed them on top of his. Rubbing his hands along my feet, he began to massage them softly.

"I tried to press charges, but there was no substantial proof that he had drugged me, even though I knew it was him. Now that I think about it, it's best that it happened four years ago rather than now because I could have been arrested for having an abortion at five months pregnant with these crazy laws Georgia got."

GQ looked at me stunned. "Word, that's crazy, damn, babe. I'm so sorry." Shaking his head, he chuckled. "I'm not laughing at you, baby. I'm just laughing at us. We are some fucked up individuals. We both have trauma. We're both dealing with it and despite all of it, we are both here, we're both fighting every day to love again. I don't know about you, but I think that's pretty dope."

"I guess you're right. I never thought about it like that," I responded

"But it's true. And you know, after I had to flee the scene earlier, all I could think about was you. Even with all the hurt for my own pride and my baby girl's heart, all I could think about was your heart, and what was going on with you, and that's when I knew—" His voice trailed off, his mouth slightly agape as he stared at me intently.

"Knew what?"

"That I love you. That what I feel for you is real. Real beyond the romance. Real beyond the infatuation and the lust. I care about you Eva, and you're the woman I want to be with."

I was blown away because I felt the exact same. The entire time he was gone, all I could think about was him, and what I would do or what I would tell Gianna if he never came back. That right there was love. True love. And it was refreshing because I hadn't felt like this in such a long time. And there was no way, I was going to hide it.

I leaned up on the couch, then straddled him, my hands were on his chin as I looked deeply into his eyes, "I love you more, baby," With the intensity of a strong tide, we kissed passionately, and I fell into his arms. For the rest of the night, we kissed, fondled, and just laid there in all of our emotional nakedness.

Loud, obnoxious bangs woke me from my sleep as I shimmed from under GQ's embrace. After making love and falling right asleep on the couch, although startled rom the impending noise , I felt well rested after all that good loving. Pulling myself off the couch as I yawned and stretched my arms, the bangs became increasingly louder. GQ was knocked out, mouth open and snoring. The fact that he hadn't woke from the noise was surprising.

I stumbled forward, walking towards the door.

"Eva, who's that banging like that on the door?"

I turned around, facing the spiral staircase and found Gianna standing there weary looking with cold planted in the crevices of her eye duct. She was wearing a bonnet and a long nightgown.

"I don't know. I'm going to see now. Head back to bed. Everything's okay."

Reluctantly, she scratched her head several times before breaking eye contact with me. Her gaze fanned over GQ. "Daddy's back. Let me wake him up."

Before I could blink, Gianna was running down the stairs, and the bangs were getting louder. I wish Gianna had listened to me and stayed upstairs. From the sounds of the bangs, a feeling in my gut just knew something wasn't right.

Finally staring at the knob I struggled to pull the heavy plank door open. Lad with hefty iron hinges, the door felt like it weighed one hundred pounds. As soon as I got it open, authorities rushed in wearing bulletproof vests, gray uniforms and AK-47s.

A short, stocky man with a bald head brushed passed me, and the steel front from his AK-47hit me in the torso area.

"Onde esta o homem da casa! "Onde esta o homem da casa!" The stocky man yelled.

Right behind him were several officers, who rushed inside.

"Babe, what's going on?" GQ's voice was a groggy high pitch.

"Get off of my Daddy!" Gianna screamed.

Before I could turn around to see what was going on, I met eyes with the beautiful woman I saw for the first time last night. She was standing on the side of the door with her husband, who had his arm draped around her waist. Dusk was among us, as the sun fought to rise, casting a colorful shadow in the air.

It felt like an eternity as me and her exchanged eye contact. Even with the bruises around her neck and the dark black ring under her left eye, her beauty still prevailed.

"You are under arrest for assault." The short, stocky bald

headed officer screamed in a thick Portuguese accent, as another officer slapped cuffs on GQ's wrist. GQ's head was down, and his shoulders slumped, as Gianna fought to break him away.

"No! Please. Please don't take my Daddy," Gianna screamed uncontrollably.

I stood still as a statue, completely lost for words. My hands were now covering my mouth, as I watch the officers trudge past, pushing GQ closer and closer to the door.

"Senorita, is this the man who assaulted you?" He asked the beautiful woman, who I now knew to be Gianna's mom.

Gina nodded sheepishly, as she tugged on her man's arm. "Yes, that's him."

To Be Continued…

connect with penny b

Stay connected with me on all platforms.

about the author

Penny Blacwrite is the #1 bestselling author of *Charlie's Angels: A Polyamorous Affair* and the award-winning poetry book *For Every Black Woman's Soul*. Also, Penny is a published journalist with credits in *Amsterdam News*, *Our Times Press*, and online entertainment publications *Parle Magazine and Enstarz*. Groomed as a student reporter from the age of twelve, Penny was trained by some of the best leading industry writers and journalists from *News Day*, *60 Minutes*, CBS, and NBC. Since then, Penny had a knack for storytelling.

As a novelist, Penny writes sexy, steamy, twisted, forbidden romances, women's fiction, and erotica. Exploring tropes like age gaps, love triangles, polyamorous relationships, secret babies, sex and romance are staple themes in Penny's work. With a catalog of twelve novels, Penny has scored ten national bestsellers and four of them have held the #1 bestselling spot for three weeks in LGBT Erotica and Black & African American Erotica. Her stories are sure to house mind-blowing secrets and finish off with an explosive ending. Nonetheless, she has always longed to tell stories that mirrored her experiences in authentic, creative ways. From being born in prison and raised as a Tupac baby to attending the illustrious Howard University, Penny's real life is the launching pad for her intricate plots, mind-blowing secrets, and explosive endings.

Penny is a New Yorker residing in New Jersey with her MacBook, and a mind full of chatter that makes for great stories. Lastly, she is currently studying for her MFA in Creative Writing where she has dreams of launching a specialized niche course focused on self-publishing and rapid releasing at an accredited university.

CLICK THE QR CODE BELOW TO STAY CONNECTED: